The Obsessed Alphas Collection

Books 1-4

Seduced by the Witness

Seducing My Wife

Seducing the Stalker

Seducing Shelly

Lacy Jane Publishing

Contents

Seduced by the Witness

Lacy Jane

Lacy Jane Publishing

Contents

Faith

♥

Worst. Day. Ever. Seriously. I slept through my alarm, tore my fingernail, broke the heel on my favorite shoes, spilled coffee down my dress, had a flat tire, and forgot to put an important meeting on my boss's calendar. I then got bitched at by my douche boss in front of the whole office. I hid out in the bathroom until I got my tears under control. Could this day get any worse? Calgon, take me away!

It's the end of the day from hell, and I'm planning to Netflix and chill, along with a blender full of margaritas. Thank God this day is done!

"Oh, shit!" I suddenly remember that I was supposed to finish typing up some very important papers for my boss. I had planned to do them at home, but forgot all about it and left all of the information I need on my desk. If I don't go pick up my paperwork tonight, my job will be toast. It might already be after all of my screwups today, but this would definitely be enough to push it over the edge.

I've worked for James, Eliot, and James, Attorneys at Law, for a year and a half. I am currently a personal assistant and, well, let's just say I really suck at it. I hate my boss, John Eliot, who has made it his personal mission in life to make snide remarks about everyone he meets. He is not a nice person. Like at all.

Even thought I'm twenty-three, I still haven't decided what I want to be when I grow up. Right now, I just want to be employed so I can eat, pay for things, and mimic being an adult.

As I pull up to the office building, I notice how dark and creepy it looks at night. I've never really noticed before because I normally leave by six. Our building is (much like Mr. Eliot) very modern and cold. Lots of angles, black and white. Absolutely no warmth. It's also very silent and filled with shadows. I just want to get the stupid papers and get the hell out of Dodge.

On the way to my desk, I notice a light coming from one of the neighboring offices. It's comforting to know that someone else is here, too. Maybe I should say hi. As I approach the door, though, I hear raised voices. I definitely do not want to interrupt whatever is going on in there.

As I pass by, I see two men. One of them is very small and frail looking. He has to be at least in his sixties. The other man is a little younger, probably mid-fifties, and looks very sinister. His eyes look cold, and I get an evil vibe from him. Enough that a shiver races down my spine.

A loud noise popping noise makes me jump. It takes a moment for my mind to register what I just heard; a gunshot. I'm frozen with fear.

"Get her!" Cold Eyes shouts. Just then, two goons that I hadn't noticed start toward me, along with Cold Eyes. The other man isn't following because he is lying dead on the floor of his office. It is just now sinking in. I just saw a man get murdered!

I race down the hall as fast as I can, sending up prayers as I go. I know I was complaining about my life just a few minutes ago, but I had really hoped it wouldn't be over for several decades. Witnessing a shooting is probably not going to help my longevity.

I slam the front door open, racing as fast as I can toward Main Street. Hopefully, people will be around and I can hide somewhere. I run for what seems like hours, but is probably only a few minutes. In the distance, I spot a police station. It's the most beautiful sight I've ever seen. "Praise the lord!"

Faith

Thank God I made it to the police station. Even better, the police don't seem to think I'm a total lunatic. Some of the officers have gone to my office building to check it out. Another sits with me while I describe the men to a sketch artist. After a while, I desperately need a break. I head to the bathroom, and happen to glance at their "most wanted" posters. I see a very familiar face.

"Holy Shit! That's Cold Eyes!"

I run back to the officer who has been helping me. I point out which man I'm talking about-Jim Rafferty. The officer looks at me with wide eyes, then takes me to a back room.

"Sit tight," he says in a very serious tone. "I have to call the Feds."

****

I've been here for a few hours now. What the hell is the deal with the Feds? What is going on? I discovered an hour ago that I am locked in this room. It makes me feel seriously claustrophobic. I just want out. I want to go home and forget about this incredibly crappy day.

I start pounding on the door and screaming like a lunatic, hoping that someone will let me out of here. "Help! Help! Let me out!" I continue pounding until my hands feel bruised. I fling myself back into my very hard chair, and lay my head down on the table.

When I finally hear the door opening, I turn around and am completely dumbstruck. The sexiest man I've ever seen struts in, sucking all the air out of my lungs.

"I'm Special Agent Evan Heart," he says, turning me into an imbecile. He's asking me things, but all I can do is stare at his sexy mouth, wondering how it would feel tasting every inch of me. Or I could taste every inch of him. Yum! Or both...

"Miss Jones?" He says in a deep voice that sends chills down my spine and moisture pooling between my legs. Good lord. What a bad time to finally have an insane, instant attraction to someone.

"I'm sorry. What did you ask?" I manage to reply.

"You are sure that the man you saw tonight was Jim Rafferty?" He asks, flashing a different picture of him.

"Absolutely," I say with certainty. "I would never forget those dead eyes."

"Well, Ms. Jones. It seems we have a problem then. You are going to have to go to a safe house until Rafferty goes to trial."

"Can't I just go home?"

"Sweetheart," he says kindly while taking both of my hands in his, totally taking my mind off the seriousness of the conversation. "All surveillance from the crime scene has magically disappeared. You are the only one who can place him there. We have been trying to nail him for years, but he has always managed to stay one step ahead of us. This is a huge break. I'm going to have one of our agents take you someplace safe, where he won't be able to find you."

"Can't you take me?" I ask, starting to panic. Besides being ridiculously good looking, Evan makes me feel safe and protected. If I have to hide out with someone, I want it to be with him.

He pauses for a moment before nodding. "Yes, sweetheart. I can do that."

Evan

♥

I'm driving to a safe house that's a couple of hours from here, up in the mountains. We have left the town of Euphoria and are headed to a tiny place called Harmony. I don't usually babysit witnesses, but this one is really important. Not only can she put a crime boss away for life; she is going to be my wife. She doesn't know that yet, of course, but as far as I'm concerned, it's a done deal. I knew the second I laid eyes on her. Mine. My heart started racing, my dick turned to stone, and I couldn't catch my breath. I have never had such a strong reaction to anyone before.

Just looking at her pale skin and long blond hair has a visceral effect on me. She is small compared to me, but who isn't? She has curves for days, though. My god. All I could do was picture sucking those luscious tits before slamming my cock all the way inside her sweet pussy. I would take her rough, and she would love every second of it. I would have her addicted to my cock in no time. Just thinking about it is not helping the steel between my legs. I can only hope that my jacket is hiding my rock hard dick.

It's not just about sex, though. I want her in every way. In my bed, in my home, in my life, having my children. I want it all. I know that until the trial is over, I have to keep my relationship with Faith professional. After that, all bets are off.

After a tortuous drive, we finally arrive at the safe house. It's a small, rundown place in the mountains. I pull inside the garage and close the door quickly. We walk inside the place that will be our home for the foreseeable future. It's surprisingly nice inside, but the outside looks like shit to keep people from being too interested in it.

"It's really cute," Faith says excitedly.

"I'm glad you are so enthused about it," I laugh. "Are you hungry? We should be fully stocked."

"I am starving. I haven't had a chance to eat eat all day," she says as her stomach rumbles. We both laugh.

We search the refrigerator and cabinets before deciding on just having sandwiches and chips. I check all the windows and doors to make sure everything is secure. Afterwards, we settle down on the couch to watch a movie. I have never watched tv with a witness before, but then again, I've never desperately wanted a witness before. I have no idea what movie is on or what has happened in it. All I am focused on is her-her creamy skin, her flaxen hair, her emerald eyes, her generous tits and ass. I shift in my seat, trying to make my poor cock more comfortable. He's been in agony since I first laid eyes on Faith, and I don't see that changing anytime soon. Not until she is finally mine. I just need to bide my time. I am in this for the long haul.

Faith

♥

Good lord, that man is sexy. Over six and a half feet of solid muscle, jet black hair with threads of gray, and chocolate eyes. He is the epitome of tall, dark, and handsome. It has taken every ounce of my self-control not to just climb his gorgeous body like a tree. I'm watching one of my favorite movies, but I haven't absorbed any of it. There's so much moisture pooling between my legs, I'm afraid I'm going to stain the sofa.

When the movie ends, Evan jumps up like the hounds of hell are on his tail. It seems he can't get away from me fast enough. I follow quietly behind him, curious about where he's going. There aren't a lot of options here. Suddenly, he spins around and slams my body against the wall.

"Jesus," he says under his breath. "I thought someone managed to get in the house."

"I'm sorry," I say quietly. He is mere inches from me. I can smell his cologne. It smells so woodsy and manly, just like him. I stare up at him and see undisguised hunger in his eyes. I lick my lips longingly. His eyes darken before he devours my lips with his.

He takes my mouth like he's starving for me. He pulls me against him, making me gasp as I feel his erection. He rubs his huge cock against my sodden pussy, just where I need it most. Even with the layers of clothing between us, it feels amazing. His hands cup my breasts and he pinches my nipples, propelling me into an unexpected orgasm. I've never been so aroused in all my life. I need him inside me now.

Suddenly, he stops and rests his forehead against mine. "Sweetheart, we can't do this," he says, taking deep breaths to get himself under control. Seriously? I may die from unrequited lust.

"What if I want to?" I say seductively, running my hands down his chest before squeezing his massive length through his pants. He is panting now, thrusting his cock into my hands. Unfortunately, he gets himself under control and sets me a few feet away from him, making me pout in disappointment.

"Baby, we will continue this, believe me, but not while I'm guarding you. I need to remain professional until then. Okay?"

I glare at him, still pouting. "Okay," I say quietly. I understand, but that doesn't mean I'm happy about it.

Faith

♥

I am a really terrible person. Like really, really terrible. I witnessed a murder, and all I can think about is Evan, who may very possibly be the sexiest man to ever walk the face of the earth.

I have gotten to know him over the last few days. Instead of finding him less appealing, I find him even more so. He has a sister, Sadie, that he feels really protective over (gee, I'd never have guessed that). He loves dogs (me, too!!!). He thinks pizza should be its own food group. He might be on to something there. I mean bread, meat, veggies, sauce, cheese. Who could ask for more?

He seems to know when we are about to get out of control again. The air will get thick between us, and he will find a reason to leave the room super fast. I don't blame him. I get it. I mean, this is his job. He can't get involved with a witness. That would look bad for him. Right now, though, I'm kind of past the point of caring. I've had a lot of bad stuff happen to me. I want something good; something just for me. I want Evan.

I've spent a lot of time daydreaming about seducing him over the last couple of days. I have all sorts of ideas, but I don't have the slightest clue what I'm doing. I've had sex once, in the dark, with my high school boyfriend. It was over really quickly and was nothing to write home about. I've never been that attracted to anyone in the past. I kind of thought there might be something wrong with me. Apparently not. I guess it just took Evan for my desire to ramp up all the way. We already had the conversation about significant others. We are both very single. The only thing in our way is his job.

I've decided to up my game. I shower and make myself look presentable. Thankfully, the safe house is stocked with a wide variety of clothing sizes. I put on a short nightgown, but don't put on any undies. I greet Evan, then make my way into the kitchen. I make sure he's watching me before I bend over to look in a cabinet. I hear a growl from him. Before I know it, he's on me. He flips me around and presses against me.

"You are playing with fire, little girl, showing me that sweet cunt. Trying to tempt me with it."

"Is it working?" I ask, suddenly breathless.

"Fuck, yes, it is," he says before slamming his lips against mine. His fingers thrust inside my pussy, making me moan. He does it harder, making moisture drip down my legs. "Do you want my big cock, little girl? Do you want me to slam it inside you and take you like an animal?"

"Yes!" His fingers fuck me harder as his lips fuck my mouth.

"I know I've been trying to keep away from you, Faith, but make no mistake. You. Are. Mine. When this shit with Rafferty is over, I'll show you how much I want you. I'll fuck your sweet little cunt every day for the rest of our lives."

With that, he takes me over the edge. I scream out my pleasure as moisture coats his fingers. "So fucking delicious," he says while licking my juices from his fingers. "We just need to hold out a little longer, baby." With that, he tugs my gown back in place and heads to his room. *Well, shit.*

****

After a very long and boring day, where Evan has kept his distance from me, I crawl into bed and try to sleep. Images of Evan keep running through my head. His mouth felt so good on mine, and his fingers. Oh my gosh! I've never come so hard in all my life. I can only imagine how good it would feel to have his cock inside me. I've felt it up against me, and it seems huge; just like the rest of him. The thought turns me on even more.

It gets hot, so I take my nightgown off. I'm soon caught up in erotic dreams about Evan. I rub my pussy harder and harder, pretending that Evan is doing it instead. I manage to come, but not like I did with him. I need the real thing. I toss and turn, finally falling into a restless sleep.

Evan

♥

I startle awake, instantly alert. I grab my gun off of the nightstand and creep silently across the hall to Faith's room. I carefully open the door, pointing my gun directly in front of me. I survey the room, but nothing seems off.

I lower the gun and set it on her nightstand. I focus on the bed now. She is asleep, but restless. The silky sheets are tangled with her legs, and she keeps twisting.

Relief sweeps through me as I realize she is just having a nightmare. I should probably wake her up, though. My dick has a lot of ideas about how he wants to handle that, but I have to remain professional. Earlier, it took everything I had not to throw Faith down on the countertop and fuck her silly after she flashed her pretty little pussy at me.

I move toward the bed slowly, trying not to startle her. She cries out. That must be what woke me up before. "Sweetheart," I say quietly, while shaking her arm slightly, like you would a child. I sit down on the edge of the bed. Suddenly, her cries sound more like those born of ecstasy than of fear. I'm afraid to move. Faith moves again, completely dislodging the covers.

My angel is now writhing around on her bed completely naked. *Jesus Christ.* I swallow hard. My imagination was bad enough, but being confronted with the flesh and blood temptation of Faith without a stitch of clothing on is more than a mere mortal should have to withstand.

"Evan, please," she moans. "I need all of you."

The hair on the back of my neck stands up and all of my blood drains into my cock. I've never been this hard in my life. If I were smart, I would walk out and forget all about this. Unfortunately, my brain is no longer running the show.

I shake her a little harder. "Faith. Wake up, honey." She opens her eyes, still looking sleepy.

"Oh, Evan," she moans sensually, "Feel how wet I am for you."

With that, she takes my hand and places it in her drenched pussy. As soon as I feel the slickness, I know that there is no way in hell I am leaving this room tonight.

I pin her body to the bed with mine and take her mouth. I kiss her lips again and again, showing her how much I want her while my fingers fuck her sweet little cunt. She's bucking now, begging for my cock. I move down and lick her pussy. It's the most delicious thing I've ever tasted. I can't get enough of her honeyed sweetness.

I suck her clit hard, and she screams, flooding my mouth with her heavenly juices. I lick up every drop. I squeeze my cock, trying to get myself under control as pre-cum drips out.

"Please, Evan! I need you now!" she says forcefully as she claws at my back. I toss my boxers off and take in her perfection. I'm going to spend the rest of my life with this woman. I lift myself over her and slam all the way in with one hard thrust. "Yes!" She screams.

"Baby, you feel so good." I've never felt anything like this before. I was certain that she was going to be mine before, but I'm even more so now. I suck her gorgeous tits and pinch her nipples hard. She seems to really like the pleasure/pain. I thrust into her wet heat again and again, wringing orgasm after orgasm from her. Every time she comes, her muscles tighten around my cock like a vise. It takes everything I have to make it last.

Finally, she comes again, almost violently, screaming so loudly she probably woke the neighbors a mile down the road. It keeps going and going. Her wetness soaks the bed and she nearly passes out. I can't hold back anymore. I slam into her even harder, making the headboard slam against the wall with the force of it. I come the hardest I ever have, spraying my seed inside her, saying a silent prayer that I get her pregnant.

"That was incredible," she says in amazement.

"That it was," I say, kissing her again. "Sleep, sweetheart," I say quietly. I pull her back against my front and hold her close to me. I hear her steady breathing, signaling she has fallen asleep, and I quickly follow.

Evan

♥

I am startled from my sleep by another noise. This time, I know that something is off. I've learned over the years to trust my instincts, and right now they are screaming at me.

"What's wrong?" Faith asks quietly.

I put my finger against my mouth, signaling that she should be quiet. She nods, but I can see the fear in her eyes. I grab my gun and creep silently toward the window. Suddenly, a black clad figure crashes through it, knocking me down.

It takes me a few seconds to recover. When I look up, the man is on his feet and pointing a gun right at Faith. She screams as I shoot him twice. His body crumples to the floor. I knock his gun away with my foot, then check his pulse. He is no longer a threat, but there will be others.

I turn my attention to Faith. Her eyes are wild and she is shaking really hard. I check to make sure no one else is here before coming back to her. "It's okay, baby," I say as I hold her. "Everything is gonna be alright."

Even as I say the words, though, I am worried. How the hell did a hit man find her here? I know that we weren't followed. The only other conclusion I can come to makes my stomach turn. There is a leak in the FBI. One thing is for certain. We need to leave right now.

"Get dressed, Faith. We have to go." When she doesn't move, I yell "now!" a bit harshly, but it jars her out of her catatonic state and gets her moving. She quickly throws on her clothes. I dress and throw her few belongings back into her bag before propelling her toward the garage and into my car. I drive away quickly, turning off the road anytime I think someone might be following us. I have to keep her safe. Not only is she the only witness who can put Rafferty away; she's also the love of my life. I just need to keep us safe long enough to get to the happily ever after part.

Evan

♥

I call Special Agent in Charge Jones and tell him what's going on. He wants to send me to another safe house. Fuck that. I am not putting Faith in any more danger than necessary. I tell him my suspicions, then let him know I'm going off the grid. I toss our phones and disable the locator on our SUV. I am well trained in how to live off the grid, I've just never actually had to do it before.

I look over at Faith and see her still shaking. "Come here, sweetheart." She moves over to the middle. I buckle her in and snuggle her against my side. "I won't let anything happen to you, baby. Not now, not ever." She must feel a little better since she closes her eyes and falls asleep.

My army buddies and I have a cabin up in the mountains. It's a few hours away, on the other side of the state. It's kept for just such a reason. No one else knows about it except Jacob, Slade, and Dax. I'd trust any of them with my life. Right now, I don't trust anyone else.

****

"Wake up, sleepyhead. We're here." Faith blinks up at me, trying to get her bearings. She looks up at the small log cabin and gets wide eyed.

"It's so beautiful," she whispers reverently. "I love it!"

I smile at her. One of the things I love about her is her enthusiasm about everything, even in the predicament she's in right now.

****

Time passes. We've been at the cabin for two weeks now. It's really not been a hardship for me. I've spent nearly every second with Faith. Since I already screwed up by sleeping with my witness, I decided to go all in and not fight it anymore.

I have fucked Faith on pretty much every surface in this cabin, and in every position imaginable. I would guess I have been inside her at least forty times. That's probably a really conservative estimate. Just thinking about her gets my dick hard again, which has pretty much become his permanent condition.

I have my former military buddies looking into who could have given up the location of the safe house to Rafferty. Everything is pointing to one man, and I hope like hell I'm wrong. Special Agent in Charge Sam Jones has been my boss for the last four years. I have trusted him completely, but I'm afraid I've made a mistake. My buddies and I put a plan in motion that will hopefully bring an end to this ordeal. Then Faith and I can begin our lives together.

Evan

My buddies have just arrived. They are giving me tons of grief.

"Oh, how the mighty have fallen," Slade says as he passes by me. The others snicker.

"What are they talking about?" Faith asks as she wraps her arms around my waist.

"Nothing," I say, taking a whiff of her hair. "It's not important, baby."

We all go over the plan together. Dax is going to take Faith somewhere safe. None of us knows where. That way, no one can be forced to talk. I hate not being with her, but I've got to button this shit up.

"Evan, I'm scared," she whispers against my chest.

"I know, baby. It will all be over soon. I promise you'll be safe. I will always protect you." I give her a very passionate kiss goodbye, only stopping when my juvenile friends start shouting "Get a room!"

"I love you, Faith." She looks at me with surprise.

"I love you, too, Evan. Please be safe." I watch her walk out with Dax, then make the call that will set everything in motion.

****

It's only been a few hours, but it seems like a lifetime. With Faith not here, I feel like a part of me is missing. I can't wait to get this shit over with. The only good thing is I am enjoying the camaraderie with my buddies. We work well together. We always did. We are reminiscing when Jacob yells "Heads up! They're here." The security equipment lights up in several places. We watch all of the cameras to see how many men we are dealing with. As expected, up walks Sam, but he's not alone.

"Son of a bitch!" I whisper loudly. Rafferty is with him. Who the hell would have expected him to show up himself instead of sending a flunky? He's really getting sloppy. He hides out around the side of the house, while Sam comes to the front door. He knocks. When I open up, he greets me warmly, like nothing is wrong. I had no idea he was such a good actor.

"Evan," he says, shaking my hand. "Great to see you, son. You've done a great job keeping the witness safe. Now how about you hand her off to me?"

I look at him and act like I am actually contemplating such a dumb ass move. "I don't know, Sam. What if they find her again?"

"Don't worry, Evan. No one will find her."

"How long have you been working for Rafferty, Sam?" The color drains from his face. He quickly recovers, though.

"What? That's just crazy. Bring me the girl."

"Her name is Faith, and no. I won't bring her to you or anyone else."

Rafferty bursts through the front door, gun drawn. "Sam, this is taking way too long. Where's the girl?" The captain looks at me. I just shrug.

"No idea." I say truthfully. Rafferty looks at me for a moment.

"Just for that, I think I'll let you watch me kill her before I kill you."
It takes everything I have not to attack him, but I know we've got to
do this shit by the book.

"Did you boys get all of that?" I ask loudly.

"Every word," says Slade, ridding Rafferty of his gun before he
knows what hit him.

I call the police and the FBI. This time, everything will be done
right. I'm mentally patting myself on the back when I hear a blast and
fall backward. I look up and see Slade drop Rafferty with one shot. I
feel a pain in my chest. *Shit.* I've been shot.

Faith

"How much longer do you think they'll be?" I ask Dax for the eighty-fifth time today. I'm surprised I haven't worn a path in the carpet. I've paced back and forth the entire time we've been in the little country house.

"It will be over soon, Faith," Dax says, not bothering to look up from his detective novel. Just when I think I might go insane, he finally gets the call. "Let's go. Evan's been shot." I try to absorb what he's telling me, but it's too much to bear. I feel a little bit dizzy, then darkness claims me.

****

I wake up in a hospital bed. *What the hell?* "You fainted," says an older man with kind eyes.

"Oh, God. What about Evan?"

"Evan is right here," my man says, rising from the chair beside my bed. "Don't worry, baby. I'm fine. It will take more than a bullet to take me from you. I had on my vest."

"Thank goodness. Rafferty?"

"He's dead, sweetheart. It's all above board and on tape. The good news is that the other men you saw that night have confessed to their part in it, and there is no longer a hit out on you. You are free to go."

"Oh," I say quietly. You would think that I would be thrilled about that, but I don't know what that means for the two of us. "What about us?" I whisper.

Evan kneels down by my bed and pops open a square box. A beautiful diamond solitaire catches the light. It's stunning. "I love you so much, Faith. I've loved you since the first time I saw you. This was my grandmother's. She wanted me to give it to "the one". That is you. Please make me the happiest man in the world and say yes."

Tears are streaming down my face, but I manage to nod my head. "Yes!" His lips descend on mine in an all-consuming kiss.

"Ahem," the doctor says, clearing his throat beside us. "I thought you might want to know your test results. Congratulations! You are pregnant." I look at Evan, who is grinning from ear to ear.

"I can't believe we are having a baby," I say to him. He grins.

"All the more reason to get you tied to me asap."

****

When he said asap, he really meant it. We flew to Las Vegas one week later, with all of those nearest and dearest to us, and tied the knot.

Epilogue-Faith-1 year later

♥

What a difference a year makes. Evan and I got married and had our baby girl, Madison, who we call Maddy for short. He quit working for the FBI, and went into business with his army buddies. They opened their own security firm, Alpha Security. They take turns working cases. Our life is happy and relaxed, and he gets to spend a lot of time with the two of us.

"There are my favorite girls," he says, walking slowly into the room and kissing Maddy's head, then my mouth.

"I missed you," I whisper against his lips. "Let me show you how much." Maddy has fallen asleep nursing. I place her in the bassinet by our bed and start undressing. My sexy husband starts shucking his clothes at record speed before pushing me down on the comforter.

"Mrs. Heart, I'm going to have my wicked way with you," he says, licking his way down my body to my needy center. His magical tongue licks and thrusts, making me lose control. I gasp, but try to be quiet. The last thing we want to do is wake the baby.

"Please, Evan. I need you."

He kisses his way up my body, devouring my mouth before finally thrusting his cock to the hilt inside of me. I cover my mouth to try to hold in my moans. He pounds into me, harder and harder. I try. I really do, but I can't hold in my scream anymore.

"Evan!" I shout as I come so hard, I nearly black out. I feel him explode inside of me seconds later. I hold him close. We chance a glance at baby Maddy, but she's still out like a light. *Thank goodness.*

"Faith, I love you so much. I love little Maddy, too. You two are the best things that have ever happened to me. I want to fill this house with babies," he says, kissing up and down my neck, causing me to get goosebumps all over.

"We are off to a great start, then," I say, looking at him expectantly.

"Are you saying?"

"Yep. We are pregnant again! I just took the test this morning."

"Holy shit! Baby, you have made me the happiest man in the world. I love you so much."

"I love you, too."

He proceeds to show me how much he loves me again before our daughter wakes up.

THE END

Seducing My Wife

Lacy Jane

Lacy Jane Publishing

Contents

Jace

♥

I take a deep breath and run my hand through my hair in agitation. I'm running on fumes these days. I'm working 70+ hours a week and sleeping (if you can call it that) at the office half the time. Let's face it-there's no reason to go home. It just reminds me of her.

Up until a month ago, I would have said my life was perfect. I was married to Chloe, who I had been madly in love with since the moment I laid eyes on her. I had a successful business, and plenty of money. What more could you ask for?

Little did I know that Chloe was unhappy. We'd been married for five years, and everything had been great. Unfortunately, over the last year, she had apparently felt like I was taking her for granted. Sure, I'd been working longer hours and coming home late more often, but the extra hours would result in a lot of extra income that would benefit both of us. Chloe is and always will be number one in my life. I thought she understood that. Apparently not.

Exactly a month ago, she walked out on me. She didn't even have the decency to talk to me about it. I came home late from work to find an empty house, cold food, and a note.

Jace,

I'm sorry, but I can't take this anymore. I love you with all my heart, but I can't continue to be a distant second to your business. You have taken me for granted for quite some time now. Tonight (our five year anniversary) was the last straw. You couldn't even get home early enough to have dinner with me. I thought it would get better, but it hasn't. Your entire focus is on your company. I know how important it is to you; I really do. I just want to be important to you, too. I feel like we need some time apart to reevaluate. I'll be in touch when I'm ready to talk.

Love,

Chloe

I had been stunned. It had never occurred to me in my wildest dreams that Chloe would ever leave me. I tried calling her, but she wouldn't answer. I kept texting her until she finally told me to stop until she was ready to talk. I stalked her to her best friend's house. After pounding on the door and standing outside yelling like a lunatic, I had to take a step back.

Not knowing what else to do, I threw myself into work even more when I wasn't drinking myself into oblivion. I looked like shit, and could probably count on one hand the hours of sleep I've gotten in the last week or two. Coffee has become my lifeblood. I need it to function.

The first week or so, I hadn't been too worried. I had figured that Chloe would be gone for a few days, then come back and everything would be fine. Unfortunately, that didn't happen. Even worse, she is now staying with her sister, Tracy, and her husband, Rick. They wouldn't let me in and their estate is a fucking fortress, so I couldn't even manage to catch a glimpse of my gorgeous wife, much less talk to her. After me repeatedly pressing their entry buzzer and trying to scale their gate, they threatened to call the police on me. That's when I knew I was out of control.

I take a moment to contemplate my next move. I need to talk to Chloe. Hell, the longest we've probably ever gone without talking before this was a day or so. I miss her. I miss everything about her. Even our house seems sad and lonely without her in it.

Our bed is enormous. I've always loved it, but it just seems so giant and empty without her. Empty, just like me. That's why I haven't even bothered trying to sleep in it since she left. I either sleep on the couch or at the office. That's not so bad, right?

My phone interrupts my thoughts as I see that my buddy, John is calling. "Hey, John. What's up?" I try to say with some enthusiasm.

"You might want to get down here. Your wife is here, and damn near every swinging dick in the place is trying to hit on her." I growl in response and am out the door before I even hang up.

Chloe

I knew this was a bad idea. After spending the last month at my sister's house being totally miserable, I decided that I needed to talk to Jace. Did I call him up? Show up at our house? No. I took the chicken shit route and came down to his buddy's bar, knowing that he would let Jace know. Not exactly the best approach, but I just couldn't bring myself to call him, even though he has been relentless in trying to reach me. I just needed some time to think. I really thought that leaving Jace might be for the best. I thought that I would feel great; whole. Instead, I'm miserable. I miss him so damn much. Damn, I do love that man a ridiculous amount.

I'm trying to enjoy my orange juice when a preppy looking drunk guy swaggers over to my table. Believe me, I don't look that great tonight, but the pickins in here are pretty slim since there are three women total, so I have gotten more than my fair share of male attention in the short time I've been here. Most of the time I can give them a death glare and they go away. It's not working on this guy, though.

"I'm really not interested," I say coolly as the man drags up a chair. "I'm very married and not looking for company."

"Oh, darlin'. That just makes it that much better. We can have a great night together with no strings," he says, licking his lips. I nearly gag at the thought of it. I'm about to light into him, when in walks my oh so sexy husband, looking really pissed.

Jace

♥

I'm driving way too fast to get to the Pig and Cow. Terrible name, I know. It's a little bar and restaurant that my best friend, John owns. I have no idea why Chloe is there. It's really a bit too seedy for her. I slam the truck into a parking space and rush to the bar. When he sees me, John nods to the back of the room. I forget to breathe.

I stare at my stunning wife and my cock hardens to the point of pain. Her jet black hair falls in waves down to her waist. Her chocolate eyes look on in irritation at the guy seating himself at her table. *Oh, hell no.* Not happening. I'm there in three strides.

"She's taken, so back the fuck off," I tell the cocky looking scumbag who's trying to hit on my woman. I can tell he wants to argue, but he hesitates. At 6'7 and 275 pounds, I'm a huge son of a bitch. I was a linebacker in college before I blew my knee out. My size intimidates most people. There are times like this that I'm happy to use it to my advantage.

"My bad," he says, putting his hands up in surrender as he walks away. I glare at him until I see him walk outside.

"Thank you," Chloe says quietly. "He didn't seem to take the hint."

I turn to face her and groan inwardly. She's got a low cut dress on that cups her generous tits lovingly. Jesus, I've missed her. I run my eyes over her curvy body, and back to her beautiful face. She licks her lips nervously, making my cock even more uncomfortable.

"Why haven't you returned any of my calls?" I ask her softly, hurt coming through in my voice.

"I'm still trying to figure out what to do. I thought we might both be happier apart, but I don't feel happy. I miss you."

I sit down and pull her onto my lap. "I miss you, too, baby," I breath in her coconut scented hair. "I miss you so much," I say, kissing her neck, then her luscious ruby lips. She returns my kiss greedily. All is right with the world again.

"My lawyer says..."

"Your lawyer?" I interrupt with steel in my voice.

"Um, yeah."

"What kind of a lawyer?"

"Well, a divorce lawyer, Jace."

"What the fuck!?" I yell, causing several people to turn in our direction. I really don't give a shit right now. "You are planning to divorce me?"

"Jace, you are making a scene," she whispers loudly.

"Oh, sweetheart. You ain't seen nothing yet," I say as I pick her curvy little body up and toss her over my shoulder.

"Let me go, you brute!" She yells, punching her fists against my back. I look up to see John laughing his ass off. I glare at him on my way out the door, but he doesn't seem to care. As we get to my truck, she's still shouting. "Put me down!" I put her down slowly, dragging her body down mine until she's breathing heavily, just like me.

"You can't divorce me, Chloe. I love you. I love you so damn much. I have been fucking miserable for the last month. You can't leave me, baby. Not for good. I'll do whatever you want. Just give me a chance; give us a chance," I say with emotion. I'm really not a crier, so I'm stunned to feel wetness on my face.

"I can't believe you are crying," she says quietly, looking like she may burst into tears herself. Chloe bites her bottom lip as she often does when she's trying to make a decision. "Okay, Jace. I'll give you a month to show me that I am important to you."

I take a deep breath. Thank God. I'm over the first hurdle, but I know I have a long way to go. "Shake on it?" she asks, thrusting her hand toward me.

"I think we can do better than that, sweetheart." I lean down and kiss her lightly. Once my lips touch hers, though, all bets are off. I pull her toward me. Her ample curves are pressed against me. Suddenly, all I can think of is getting inside her. It's been over a month, and I am starving for her. I lift her up and put my lips on hers again, devouring them. She moans into my mouth and melts against me, clawing at my back. My other hand goes under her dress, cupping her pussy. She cries out against my mouth. She is so wet, she is dripping with need. I move her lacy panties to the side and fuck her with my fingers. First one, then two, then finally three. She cries out and gushes ever few pumps. I am so far gone. There is no way I am stopping this.

In one quick motion, I unzip my jeans, pull out my massive cock and slam it deep inside her. She screams out in ecstasy as she comes on my cock over and over again. She's so hot and tight. I can barely hold on, but I want this to last as long as possible. I hold her up with my arms, impaling her over and over again on my steel rod.

The sound of voices floats over to us, bringing us back to reality. I open the back door of my truck. I'm still buried inside her as she wraps her legs around my waist. "Don't stop, Jace."

"Believe me, sweetheart, that's the last thing I'm gonna do." I lay her down on the backseat, pull the door shut, and slam into her with everything I've got. Sweat is dripping down my face. All I care about is fucking my wife, reminding her that she is mine.

The seat is a mess with Chloe's wetness. God, it's so hot when she comes. She doesn't just have orgasms, she has liquid orgasms and so many that we can never keep count. I've never know any other woman to do what she does, and it turns me the fuck on every time.

"You! Are! Mine!" I say with each slam of my hips. "Say it!"

"I'm yours. Every part of me belongs to you. Please fuck me harder, Jace." I speed up, giving her exactly what she is asking for, what she wants; all of me. No woman before was ever able to take all of me, but Chloe has since day one. She's a tiny thing, but she happily takes all ten inches of my thick cock.

I feel my release slamming through me. With a yell, I slam into her one last time, shooting rope after rope of cum inside her, marking her as mine. We both struggle to catch our breath. I collapse against her, raining kisses down her face and neck.

"Come home, baby doll," I whisper against her ear.

"No."

"She said no?" my brother, Sam asks incredulously. I nod my head in the affirmative. I asked him over to have someone to talk to. He's the most sensible person I know, as well as one of my best friends. I need someone to make sense of this.

"Hell. She had been thinking about serving me divorce papers, but decided to give me a month to prove how important she is to me." She then gave me a quick kiss with a promise to start answering my calls, texts, and visits. The ball was now firmly in my court.

Sam lets out a loud whistle. "Damn. So now what are you going to do?"

"Beats the hell out of me, but I've got to do something. Something big."

****

The next day, I send her a dozen long stemmed roses, along with a note:

You are my breath.
You are my pulse.
You are my life.
You are my love.

I need you.

I love you.

Forever.

Jace

I send flowers every day for the next week, and send her texts. We even start talking nightly. We dance around sore subjects; afraid to bring up anything controversial. On Friday, I finally talk her into going out on a full-fledged date with me.

I pull into her sister's drive right before seven. I practically sprint up the steps. Before I can knock, Chloe opens the door, taking my breath away. Her black lace dress is molded to her body, emphasizing every one of her gorgeous curves. Her hair is piled on top of her head in some sort of updo. She looks absolutely stunning, and I am as hard as a fucking rock.

"Hi," she says shyly.

"Hi yourself," I say in a gravelly voice. "You look beautiful."

"Thank you," she says smiling at me.

I help her into my truck and head toward her favorite restaurant, Nepal's. It's an Italian place that we used to go to on a regular basis, but haven't been to in months. She seems pleasantly surprised when I pull into the parking lot.

I help her out of the truck, pulling her up against me. I take a breath. It takes every bit of my self-control not to fuck her against my vehicle again. She leans up and kisses me. It starts off softly, then spirals completely out of control. We devour each other with our mouths and tongues. I press against her, thrusting my cock against her pussy. We are both moaning and rocking against each other. A car pulling in startles us, and we jump apart, laughing hysterically. After taking several deep breaths, we pull ourselves together and head into the restaurant.

Dinner is pretty comfortable overall. The only thing that quickly seems to turn her mood south is when my company is brought up. I quickly change the subject to my family, who all miss her deeply. She smiles sadly, and I know she misses them just as much.

After dinner, I drive us home. I don't really give it much thought. This is where we live, after all. Unfortunately, Chloe is not having it. "What the hell?" She asks heatedly.

"Baby, this is our home."

"I haven't lived here for a while. Please take me home to my sister."

"No!" She turns to glare at me. "I'm not trying to be an asshole. I swear. If we are going to give this a chance, we need to live together," I say, knowing that there is no way in hell I am letting her go.

"But no sex, right?"

I can't help it. I start laughing so hard, tears are running down my face. Her glare gets even scarier. I force myself to stop. "Sorry, babe. Hell. We could barely make it through dinner tonight without jumping each other. Sex is non-negotiable."

"But you won't force me, right?"

This time, I'm the one who's pissed. "When in the fuck have I ever forced myself on you?"

"I'm sorry. You're right. But that doesn't mean we're having sex."

"Whatever you say, princess."

****

Later that night, she tries to sleep in one of the guest rooms. Once again, not happening. She squeals as I pick her up and toss her onto our bed. "Okay," she says hesitantly. " I will sleep in the same bed as you as long as you promise to be on your best behavior."

"Done," I agree, since that could be interpreted in a lot of different ways. She gets ready for bed, and finally emerges with sweats and a huge shirt on. "What the fuck?" I look at her questioningly. "You have never slept with a stitch of clothing on. You have always slept naked with me. Always."

"Well, that was before, so that I could sleep as close to you as possible, and for easy access. Now we don't need that."

"The hell we don't," I say, stripping her clothes off. She starts to object, but doesn't put up much of a fight. I've been with her long enough to read her reactions. Her heavy breathing and dilated eyes tell me she's turned on; not to mention her rock hard nipples. I suck one chocolate nipple into my mouth, then the other. I squeeze and rub her huge breasts, which seem even bigger than I remember. I then kiss down her body until I reach her drenched pussy.

Damn, she tastes delicious. Her honey tastes even sweeter than I remember, if that's possible. I lick her lightly at first, then harder. I fuck her with my tongue and fingers, making her squirm. I suck her clit into my mouth and she explodes, drenching my face.

After giving her a second to catch her breath, I work my way up her body, giving her a soft kiss that turns feral. I'm so damn hungry for her that I've turned into an animal. I put my weight on her and feel her gasp against my mouth. My cock is as hard as a rock and is right up against her pussy. Her hot, dripping wet pussy. "Chloe?" I ask, since I said I wouldn't force the matter.

"Yes. I don't want to fight this. I need you inside me," she purrs. "Fuck me. Please, Jace. I need you." She is so wet for me that she's dripping on the bed. It's taking everything I have not to just rut in her like a wild animal. Finally, when she's writhing underneath me, I slam my steel rod all the way in, causing us both to gasp.

"Jesus, Chloe. You feel so fucking good."

"So do you, Jace. Please don't stop. Harder. Please. Fuck me harder. Don't hold back."

That's all I need. I let go, holding out as long as I can as I drive again and again into her scorching heat. When she screams out her release, I let go as her pussy milks every drop of cum from me. We both lay there for several minutes trying to catch our breath. Damn, that was good. But, then again, It always has been. We might have problems, but sex is not one of them. I think back to when I first saw Chloe...

I was out with the guys, celebrating Sam's promotion. We were walking into O'Shea's bar when someone slammed into me. I instinctively caught her to catch her from falling.

"I'm so sorry," a sultry voice said.

The beauty looked up at me, and I knew my whole world had just changed. She was the most stunning woman I'd ever seen, but it was more than that. Five feet nothing of curves with the most beautiful chocolate eyes I'd ever seen and a cute brunette bob. She was cute, sexy, and sassy. As soon as I saw her, visions of our life together played like a movie in my head-her with our children, with me in bed, laughing. I knew then and there that she was mine.

"I'm Jace Hunter," I said, kissing her hand. Electricity zipped up my arm, reinforcing my feelings. "The future father of your children."

She looked up at me and laughed. "I'm Chloe. That may be the most original line I've ever heard. Does it normally work?"

"I've never used it before-I swear. It's not a line, sweetheart. It's the truth. You were meant to be mine."

"Wow. You are cocky, aren't you?"

"Not cocky. Just certain."

With that, I bent down and kissed her; first with my mouth, but soon with my whole body. Now that I think about it, I'm really lucky that she didn't slap me or worse. It would have been warranted, really. After several minutes of kissing, I pulled back. She was breathing heavily and looked just as dazed as I felt.

"Would you like a drink?" I asked, determined to keep her with me.

"Yes," she said quietly, touching her swollen lips. We talked for the next hour, brushing against each other, and dancing around what was happening between us.

"Come home with me," I breathed against her ear, feeling her shiver.

"Yes." With that one word, I picked her up and carried her out of the bar. I settled her in my truck before giving her a couple of barely leashed kisses. I gripped the steering wheel, trying to control myself until we got home.

When we finally pulled into my drive, she looked around with awe. "This is beautiful, Jace."

"Thank you. I hope you'll like living here." She giggled again, not realizing I was totally serious. Her place was now here with me. She was where she belonged. I sounded nuts, but that's the way it was.

I barely had her in the door before we were tearing each other's clothes off. She jumped and wrapped her legs around my waist and kissed me with everything she had. I knew I was a goner. I made it all the way to the couch before devouring her. There's no way I could make it to the bed. I kissed every inch of her body while undressing her. Her body was thrusting and moving. She made the sexiest little moans I had ever heard. After teasing her incessantly, I ripped her little pink panties right off her body and fused my mouth to her pussy.

"Oh my god!" she cried while bucking against my face. I held her down and devoured her. Every time I sucked her clit, I was rewarded with a gush of her juices.

"Jace," she said breathlessly, "I really need to tell you something. I've never done this before."

I took a deep breath. How was that even possible? No other man had ever known her sweetness, and now they never would. The Neanderthal in me was thrilled. She was mine. Only mine.

"I need to get you ready for my cock, sweetheart," I said, scissoring my fingers inside her sweet pussy. "Your sweet little cunt is going to have to loosen up to take all of me."

She gushed again. I was already learning her body. I could tell she liked it when I talked dirty. She was fucking perfect. I finally unzipped my jeans, letting my cock breathe. It bounced up past my belly button, already oozing pre-cum. I laid her down on the couch, and inched inside her heat.

"Yesss," she hissed. I tried to take it slowly, but it was killing me. I had never wanted anyone so much in my life. "Please, Jace. Push all the way in." With that, I pushed past her barrier, sealing her fate. She sucked in a loud breath, and her eyes became huge.

"Fuck!" I cried out. I was all the way in her tight cunt. It was squeezing the life out of me, and nothing had ever felt so good. I stayed still for several seconds, giving her time to recover and trying to keep myself from blowing.

"Please, Jace. Don't hold back. Fuck me as hard as you want to."

"You are so fucking perfect," I breathed against her mouth as I slammed my cock in and out of her, again and again. I had never been so out of control, but she loved it. She screamed and gushed again and again. Finally, I couldn't hold back any longer and filled her with cum. I knew that she was my home now. I had never come so hard in my life. I felt like I might pass out. We laid on the couch for several minutes catching our breath, before I picked her up bridal style and took her to my bedroom.

She spent the night. I took her over and over again. We stayed up all night talking and fucking. I knew that there was no way I could ever let her go. I flew her to Vegas the next day and married her before the weekend was up. Crazy, I know. But when your know, you know. Why wait?

I come back to the present, and look over at her beautiful face. She is exhausted. I pull the covers over her, and she instinctively curls into my body. I know that she loves me just as much as I love her. I've just got to convince her to stay.

Jace

♥

I'm in my office, pacing back and forth. I need to find a way to spend less time working. Chloe is the most important thing in my life. I cannot lose her, no matter what I have to do. I call Sam in to talk again. I could use some feedback.

"I'm selling the company." Sam looks shell shocked. Probably because outside of Chloe, I really have no other interests. My work is my life, to the extent that it's affecting my home life. I know this is what needs to be done, and I am good with it.

"Hey, man. Whatever makes you happy," he offers with a smile.

****

I've built the most successful realty company in the state. Hunter Sells is a household name. I've put my heart and soul into it, but I'm ready for a new chapter in my life. I make some calls to parties that might be interested in buying me out. I talk to several. Now I just have to wait and see who bites.

I make sure to leave work at five. I am determined to do that every day so that Chloe can't say I'm spending too much time at work. I walk in the door at fifteen after and she looks stunned.

"You're home?" she questions, stating the obvious.

"I told you I would make sure you know you are my number one priority, sweetheart. I'm even taking a three day weekend."

"Are you serious?" She asks. At my nod, she bursts into tears.

"Baby. Whatever I did, I'm sorry."

She laughs through her tears. "Jace, I'm just so happy that you are taking this seriously."

I pull her close and hold her, inhaling the coconut smell of her hair. I tilt her face up so that she can see the determination on my face. "I can't lose you, Chloe. You are everything to me. Nothing else matters without you. I love you so much, babe."

She hugs me tightly. "I love you, too," she whispers.

Chloe

♥

It has been two weeks since I came back home. Jace really has been paying a lot more attention to me. He has been home at a decent time every night, and we've spent lots of quality time together. We talk, watch tv, make love. He seems to be all in, thank God.

He left for work a while ago. I'm still lying in bed. Every time I try to get up, the room starts spinning. So far, pregnancy sucks. Just saying. My sister says it's because I've been so stressed out. That is totally possible, I suppose. I need to tell Jace, but I want to work things out between us before I tell him that our lives are about to completely change.

It's a good thing that I'm a web designer, so I already work from home. There is no way I could make it into an office every day feeling like I do right now. I order a smoothie and some bagels to be delivered. Thank God for DoorDash! I am lightheaded, but I am also absolutely starving.

I manage to make it out of bed and to the front door to retrieve my goodies. By the time I have two of my cinnamon crunch bagels (don't judge), I feel much better. I am still getting ready when Jace shows up unexpectedly.

"Hey, babe," he says, giving me a quick kiss on the mouth which quickly escalates. We both step back after several seconds, breathing very hard.

"Did you forget something?" I ask. It is only ten in the morning, after all.

"Not at all," he tells me happily. "Get dressed. I have a surprise for you."

"Okay," I say suspiciously. "What is it?"

"Babe, that's not how surprises work."

"Fine. Let me get dressed," I pout.

A short while later, we are driving out of the city to our mystery destination.

"Are we going on a trip?" I ask. Jace shakes his head no.

"Just relax. Lie back and rest. We'll be in the car for a little bit."

I take his advice and nod off almost immediately, dreaming about the tiny person in my womb that will look like both of us.

Chloe

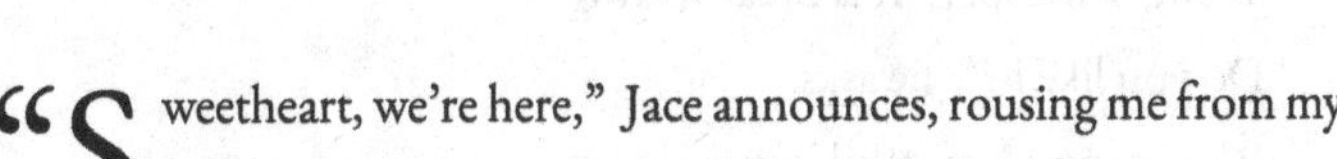

"**S**weetheart, we're here," Jace announces, rousing me from my nap.

"How long was I out?"

"Almost two hours. Did you not sleep well last night?" He asks with concern.

I feel so bad not telling him about the baby. It's on the tip of my tongue, but I freeze and just agree.

I feel bad lying to Jace (It's only a fib! I only agreed that I didn't sleep well last night). I really need to come clean. I square my shoulders and take a deep breath, thinking about what I want to say. Just as I'm about to start, I look up and am stunned into silence.

We are at Jasmine House. It's a gorgeous cottage a couple of hours outside the city. It's my absolute dream home. Not long after we got married, I told Jace I wanted to live there someday. Not that realistic a dream, but I couldn't help it. The place is to die for.

"What on earth are we doing here?" I ask, looking around the beautiful grounds. Everything is so lovely. When I said a cottage, I probably understated it. It's gigantic, but it seems very homey and quaint. Not at all pretentious. The perfect place to raise a family.

He shoots me a mysterious smile, raises his eyebrows dramatically, and pulls me toward the door and opens it with a key.

"Where did you get that? Do we get a private tour?" I ask excitedly. I've always wanted to see all of the rooms. What a great surprise!

He laughs. "You could say that," he says, steering me through the house. I gasp as we walk inside the massive great room. There is a floor to ceiling fireplace, rough sawn wood beams across the ceiling, and a stunning kitchen that could belong to a professional chef. The ceiling is at least twenty feet tall.

"Wow," I whisper. It is breathtaking.

"Do you like it?" he asks.

"It's the most beautiful house I've ever seen," I say reverently.

"I'm glad you like it, babe, because it's ours."

"What? Are you serious?"

"Yes, baby." I'm shocked speechless. My eyes fill with tears and overflow down my cheeks. "Please tell me these are happy tears," he says quietly.

"You know they are!" I laugh, trying to wipe the tears away. "I can't believe you did this! So will we live here on the weekends?"

"No, babe. That's the other part of the surprise. I'm selling my company. We can live here full time, and raise our family here; just like you wanted."

Now the tears are really flowing. "I don't know what to say. I hate for you to give up your company. You love your work."

He corrects me. "No. Once upon a time I did. I really haven't loved it for a long time. I love you. I want you to be happy. I think this will be good for both of us. What do you say? Have I convinced you to stay?"

I smile through my tears. "Definitely!" I say, throwing myself into his arms.

"Forever?"

"Forever."

He shoots me a devilish smile. "Maybe we need to start trying to make our first baby. We have a lot of rooms to fill up."

"About that," I look at him nervously. "Please don't be mad at me for not telling you sooner. I'm three months pregnant. Surprise!" I say, praying that he won't be angry.

"Are you serious?" he asks quietly. At my nod, moisture gathers in his eyes. "Oh, baby. You already make me the happiest man in the world, and now you are making me a father. I love you so much," he says, kissing me passionately. As he draws back, I smile up at him. "You know, even though you are already pregnant, we really do need to start on christening all of the rooms," he grins mischievously.

"Absolutely," I say as he picks me up bridal style and carries me up the stairs to our new bedroom.

As he lowers me to the floor, I quickly undo his slacks. I kneel down on the bed because he is so much taller than me. I push his pants and boxers down his hips and suck the head of his cock into my mouth.

"Chloe, baby, that feels so good," he moans.

I look up at him. He loves to watch me do this. I lick around the crown before taking him nearly all the way in. His cock hits my throat, but, thankfully, doesn't seem to make me sick. He tastes delicious, and it makes me suck him harder.

After a few minutes, he pulls me off and flips me to my hands and knees. He slams into me fully. He's totally out of control, and I love it. He fucks me harder than ever. I love every second of it. I feel my orgasm through my entire body. Our cries are loud as we come together, christening our new bedroom. It only takes us a few days to christen every room in the house.

Jace-Epilogue

♥

One year later...

I can't believe I am sitting here holding my baby girl, Josalyn. Out of all the gifts my wife has given me, she is the best. One look at her, and I knew I would be wrapped around her finger for life. She coos up at me. She looks just like her mom. Gorgeous. One day, I will have to scare the shit out of any boys who sniff around her, but right now I just need to love her.

Uh-oh. She's starting to get that look. "Chloe!" I yell, knowing what's coming next. Josalyn scrunches up her face and starts crying loud enough to wake the dead. Thankfully, Chloe comes in just in time.

"Poor baby," she coos to our little one. "Are you hungry?" She takes Josalyn from me, settling her against her breast to nurse. She latches on and her crying stops immediately.

As I watch my girls, I think about how much our lives have changed over the last year. Nowadays, I work, but in moderation. I act as a consultant, and mainly from my office at home. That leaves me much more time with my girls.

Chloe was designing websites, but now she is writing mystery novels instead. She decided her heart really wasn't in web design. She just finished her first book and is shopping it around to publishers. I know I might be biased, but I really do think it is fantastic. She is not only beautiful; she's brilliant.

Another thing about my wife-she was born to be a mother. She never seems stressed or upset with little Josalyn. She is so patient, loving, and kind with both of us. You can feel the love when the two of them look at each other.

I put my arms around the two of them. "I love you both so much," I say, raining kisses down on the two of them, sending Chloe into a fit of giggles.

"We love you, too," Chloe says dreamily.

Chloe and Josalyn are not only the most important people in my world; they are my world. I don't know how I got so lucky, but I'm so glad I did. Nearly losing Chloe was a much needed wake up call. Now I make sure to tell her with words and actions every day how much I love her and how important she is to me. She and our little girl are the best things that have ever happened to me, and I will make sure to never take either of them for granted.

THE END

Seducing Her Stalker

Lacy Jane

Lacy Jane Publishing

Contents

Jax

♥

Main Street is full of activity. People walk to work, but no one is in a hurry. Everyone smiles and greets each other. Everyone is friendly, and no one is scared. Nestled at the foot of the Rockies, Lucky Springs, Colorado looks like something out of the fifties with all the mom and pop stores lining the street.

As I'm driving by, a tiny blonde goddess with pinup curves turns and smiles. The air leaves my lungs and my heart nearly beats out of my chest. She is the most stunning creature I've ever laid eyes on. She's standing on the sidewalk in front of the local coffee shop talking to another girl. She has no idea that both of our lives are about to change.

My body is on high alert, and my cock is hard as a rock and pulsing; straining to break through the zipper of my jeans. *Jesus.* I have never had this kind of reaction to a woman in my life. I haven't even talked to her, and I already know that I would do anything to make her mine. My caveman instincts kick in, making me want to toss her over my shoulder and kidnap her; keeping her hidden away forever.

Her bobbed flaxen hair blows around her perfect porcelain face. Her emerald eyes glitter with happiness as she takes a sip of her drink. Her puffy lips touch the cup, making me jealous of it. She is dressed conservatively in a blue dress that covers her from head to toe, but there is no hiding her luscious curves.

She tells the girl walking with her goodbye as she hurries inside the town library. I have no idea who she is, but I will. She has instantly become my number one priority in life. If I had my way, I'd fly her to Vegas right this second and she'd be Mrs. Jaxon Stone by the end of the night.

It's my first day here and I've managed to find my soul mate. What are the odds? My Army buddies have been telling me all about this town for quite some time. One by one, they moved out here. First Evan moved here with his wife, Faith. Not too long after that, Jacob, Dax, and Slade followed. After a few months, they ganged up on me and convinced me to move here, too.

The five of us have always worked well together. We had all been out of the army for a short while when we came to the realization that we hated our jobs. One night, after a lot of drinking, we decided we should all ditch our respective jobs and start a security company together, since that was our area of expertise. Soon after, Alpha Security was formed.

Since I mainly do computer work, I can work from just about anywhere. I was living near Ft. Bragg, North Carolina, where we had been stationed, when the guys convinced me to move. Evan kept saying there was something in the water here. He knew several single men, himself included, who had fallen victim to love at first sight. I thought he was full of shit until I laid eyes on my little angel a few minutes ago. I already know I would do anything for her. But first, I need to find out all about her.

****

Thankfully, in a town this size and with my connections, it doesn't take long to find out about my little goddess. Serena Scott. Twenty-two. Recent college graduate and assistant librarian for the Lucky Springs Library. She lives at 1721 Maple Street.

As luck would have it, I am supposed to look at houses today, and I will definitely be finding a place close to where she lives. I can't bear to be away from her. I am already that obsessed.

I call up my realtor and give him instructions to find something as close as possible to her address. A short while later, he calls me up. My some miracle, there is a house for sale right across the street from hers. I put an offer on it sight unseen. I take it as a sign from the universe that I am supposed to be with Serena when the owners agree to my offer. I am on my way to being a homeowner and (more importantly) closer to my angel.

Serena

I am drinking my cappuccino, when the hairs on the back of my neck stand up. I have goosebumps and suddenly feel warm all over. It feels like someone is watching me. It's nuts, of course. There are lots of pretty girls here, and I'm not anything special to look at. I'm more girl next door than femme fatale. I am short, curvy, and generally referred to as "cute". Why would anyone be watching me? I'm just a quiet bookworm in a small mountain town. My imagination is obviously working overtime.

I say goodbye to my friend, Emily, and race up the street to work. If I don't get to the library before eight, old Ms. Minny will have a conniption. When you think of the stereotypical matronly librarian with glasses, gray hair, and a dress buttoned to the top of her neck, I swear it is her. She looks ninety, but has to be decades younger than that.

Today is a pretty typical October day. It's a little chilly, so all of our programs for the day are inside. The preschool bring the kids over for story time, which is my favorite. I read to the little ones while they watch me; spellbound by the tales I tell. This is why I wanted to be a librarian. Books can take you anywhere your imagination can go.

A darling little girl named Susie plops herself into my lap while I read. She is so adorable with her toothy grin, I feel my biological clock kicking to life. I love kids; I really do. Someday, I hope to have some of my own. The problem is, I kind of need a man for that, and I don't know of anyone in our small town that I would even want to have coffee with, much less children.

Just as I'm lamenting the lack of available baby daddies in Lucky Springs, the front door opens, revealing the hottest male specimen I've ever seen. The breath whooshes out of my lungs, forcing me to concentrate on getting enough air. Holy shit! This man is fine! Tall, dark, tatted, muscled up, and drop dead sexy.

"Hi there," he rasps. Oh, God. I feel my nipples pebble and my panties drench. My whole body is on high alert. My reaction to this man is overwhelming. His whiskey colored eyes rake over me, making me even warmer. I hope he likes what he sees. I know that I do.

His silky dark hair is short, but oh, so sexy, along with his neatly trimmed beard. I've never given beards any thought one way or the other, but I can't help but picture his rubbing against my pussy, which pulses as I think about it.

As he walks up to the front desk, I have to crane my neck to look up at him. Good lord. I realize I am pint sized at five two, but he must be easily six and a half feet tall, with enough muscles to make an NFL player jealous.

"Hi. How may I help you?" I manage in my best librarian voice. *Our kids would be so beautiful...*

He smiles. "I'm new in town. My name is Jaxon Stone. Everyone calls me Jax. I work for Alpha Security. I just came by to introduce myself and leave my card. If there's anything I can do for you, just let me know."

So many things. "I'm Serena Scott. It's very nice to meet you," I say, taking his hand. It dwarfs mine. Just a simple touch is sending zings all over my body. And his smell...yum. I just want to sniff him all over. His cologne makes me think of dark nights and sex. I need to get my mind out of the gutter. "I hope you'll like it here. It's a great place to live."

"I love it here already." He proceeds to tell me a bit about his security company. I have met a couple of his business partners in passing. He talks to me for several minutes, even asking my opinion on several of the latest bestsellers before turning to leave. "It was very nice to meet you, Serena. I'll see you soon," he smiles and winks.

I turn the card over in my hand. "You bet you will," I whisper at his back. He walks out the door, giving me a view of the finest backside I've ever seen. Our little town just got a whole lot more interesting.

Jax

♥

Money talks. No matter what people tell you, you can make just about anything happen with enough money. That's why right now, I am moving into my new house only a few days after putting an offer on it.

Between socking away most of my money earned in the Army plus what I inherited when my folks passed away, I have plenty. I could get by without working, but I'd probably be bored to tears in no time at all. The good news is money isn't an issue, so I am able to buy the house across from Serena's with no problem, and give them a bonus to let me live there until I close on it.

I didn't want to waste any time getting back to my angel. Now I understand how my buddy, Evan must have felt when he met his wife, Faith. He said that the second he laid eyes on her, he was a goner. The second I saw Serena, I was, too. I have dated from time to time, but I haven't really had a girlfriend before, and I've never thought about marriage. I was never opposed to it; I just hadn't met anyone that I would want to spend the rest of my life with. That all changed when I laid eyes on her. I would happily wife her up today if she would let me.

"Jax?" she calls from her front yard.

"Hey, Serena. What are you doing here?" I ask, feigning surprise.

"I live here," she motions to the large white house behind her. "What are you doing here?"

"I am moving into the house across the street."

"No way! The Anderson's place? That's awesome!" she gushes. Her bountiful tits bounce up and down as she jogs over to me. The t-shirt and short shorts she is wearing don't cover nearly enough of her curves. Not that I don't want to see every inch of her delicious body. I just don't want anyone else seeing it. She launches herself at me, nearly knocking me down, as she hugs me.

I take a deep whiff of her coconut scented hair, and feel my cock stiffen uncomfortably. I try to hold her far enough away that she doesn't see what a pervert I truly am. I try running baseball stats in my head, and anything else I can think of to keep my mind off of the beauty in front of me. Unfortunately, nothing seems to work. The good news is I have lots of boxes to hide my condition behind.

"Welcome to the neighborhood. I'm so glad you are here," she smiles at me. Damn, she's beautiful. Her smile could light up the entire fucking planet. I need to see it twenty-four-seven.

"Me, too, sweetheart. Me, too. So, how long have you lived here?"

"Oh, gosh. All of my life."

"Maybe you can show me around sometime."

"I would love to."

"Do you live here alone?"

"No." The possessive beast inside of me wants to scream. Of course someone as gorgeous as she is has someone, though it wasn't mentioned in the quick background check I did on her.

"Boyfriend? Husband?" I growl, already plotting how to get rid of whoever is in the way of me claiming my little angel.

She laughs. "No, silly. I still live with my parents. They are out of town on an extended second honeymoon. I lived at home while I went to college, and just graduated a few months ago. I suppose I should move out on my own, but I just haven't had much reason to."

I'll give her a reason to move out. I plan on being balls deep inside her sweet little pussy constantly. She'll need to move in with me as soon as possible so that no one can hear her screams as I fuck her all night every night. I just need to convince her of that.

<h1 style="text-align:center">Serena</h1>

♥

I can't believe Jax is going to be living across the street from me. The first time I saw him, I nearly hyperventilated. He has the whole tall, dark, and handsome thing going on in spades. The ebony hair, tan skin, and mountain of muscles work for him, and they definitely work for me. When I gave him a hug today, I drenched my panties just from having my arms around him. Who knows what I would do if he ever kissed me. I would probably climb him like a tree and beg to ride his big cock.

Who am I kidding? A big, sexy man like Jax would never be interested in someone like me. I am the shy, quiet girl that most people don't even notice. I don't do well in crowds. Some people think I'm stuck up, but I just have a really tough time talking to people unless it's about books. Or, I should say, I usually do. Something about Jax makes it easy. Even though we just met, it feels like I've known him forever. I think I would feel comfortable talking to him about anything, with the exception of telling him that I'm madly in love and lust with him and want to have his babies as soon as humanly possible.

I walk inside my bedroom and lie down on the fluffy pink comforter. As I think about Jax, I move my fingers across my pussy. Just from that little encounter, I am absolutely drenched. Before long, I have tossed off my shorts and am working my fingers inside, imagining his big cock instead. I mean, the man is huge, so it's pretty safe to assume he's big all over. Yum.

I'm really inexperienced, considering I've never had sex with anyone. Jax, on the other hand, is older and probably very experienced. I mean, just look at him. He could have any woman he wants. I've always cared way more about books than boys or, I should say, I did. Since I first met Jax, he is all I can think about, to an unhealthy degree.

I imagine us out on dates, kissing, having sex, getting married, and having babies. Yes, I do realize that I'm getting way ahead of myself here. He hasn't even asked me out, and probably won't. A girl can dream, though.

I've only had a few orgasms before, and always by my own hand. It isn't usually easy for me; even with my very vivid imagination. There's something about Jax, though. Just the thought of his big, hard body and handsome face makes me wet. I want him so much. I move my fingers over my swollen clit as I picture him taking what he wants from me; pounding me hard. I cry out, coming so hard I get dizzy. If I could only have the real thing.

Jax

❤

I watch Serena's sexy ass sway as she walks the three blocks to the library. She will stop at the coffee shop for a few minutes, then head to work. I know this because I have been following her for the last few days. Not because I'm obsessed with her; because I'm making sure she is safe. This is the lie I keep telling myself to justify stalking her every day, even though the crime rate in Lucky Springs is practically nonexistent.

She turns around quickly like she senses me. I duck behind a building for a second. When I peer around the corner, she is making her way up the library steps. Damn. That was close. I must be losing my edge. I've never had anyone make me in all the times I've done surveillance. Of course, it could be because it is so personal this time.

I stop by the library to see her and pick up a new thriller to read. I only ever get one at a time so I'll have a reason to come by again soon. Serena shines her beautiful smile at me, feeding my obsession. If she knew how fixated I was on her, she would run from me in terror.

I leave, only to spend part of the day in my car, watching her. This is what I do. Every single day. She is my obsession. I need to be able to see her at all times.

Serena

♥

The first time I thought Jax was following me, I figured it was just my imagination working overtime. Now, though, I'm beginning to wonder. He has followed me to work for the last few days. This, I know for certain. I've been very sneaky with my sleuthing. I have stopped to look at my hair in store windows and seen him following behind me. Even before I saw him, I sensed him. I know it sounds nuts, but my body lights up like a pinball machine whenever he is close by.

He is in the library again. You would think between moving in and working, he wouldn't have time to hang out here in the middle of the day, but he does. Every. Single. Day. My nipples tighten every time I hear that deep, sexy voice, and I have pretty much ruined all of the panties I have worn this week. I've had to start checking my bras each morning. I have to wear thicker ones so that my hard nipples don't give away my reaction every time I see him.

This man is so delicious. Even his name is sexy. *Jaxon Stone.* Just imagine how good Serena Stone would sound. The fact that he is following me has to mean something. I would never think an older, sexier guy like him would be interested in me, but he must be. Why else would he follow me?

I told my friend, Savannah about him. She volunteers at the library from time to time. She has become my partner in crime this week, staying on the lookout for my hunk. She rushes in; breathless from the cold. "Serena, your guy is parked across the street watching you again."

"Really?"

"I know he's hot and all, but do you not think it's a little creepy that he's so obsessed with you?"

"No. I should, but I don't. Besides, we don't know that he's *obsessed* with me. Maybe he just finds me interesting. Who knows? I've never been followed by anyone before. It's more than a little flattering; especially when that someone is Jax."

She laughs. "He is pretty dreamy. Just don't end up as a story on Dateline. Okay?"

"Promise," I laugh, doing a pinky swear like we've done since kindergarten.

Jax

♥

My bedroom faces Serena's. I don't think she realizes that. If she did, she wouldn't be putting on a show for me. She walks to the bathroom, taking off clothing as she goes until she's down to a black G-string and lacy black bra. Good lord. My buttoned up little librarian wears some sexy fucking lingerie under her clothes. My heavy breathing is fogging up the window. Her supple curves are enough to tempt a saint, and believe me, I'm not one.

She unhooks her bra, giving me a fleeting glimpse of the most perfect tits ever made, before walking out of the room. Damn. My cock begs for release. I jerk myself off in seconds just remembering how good she looked. It doesn't help. No matter how many times I take myself in hand, I'm still hard as a rock whenever she is near.

I know I'm not good enough for her. I'm too old, too jaded, and too rough. It doesn't seem to matter, though. I'm so obsessed with her; I can't focus on anything else. I have to have her; the sooner the better.

****

The next day, after following her to work, I head back to her house. The security there is a joke. I really need to talk to her and her parents about it. I don't even have to break in. The back door is unlocked, not to mention there is a key to the front door under the flower pot. *Jesus.* I know we live in a pretty safe town, but criminals are everywhere. I've got to protect my angel.

I take a look around the home Serena was raised in. There are lots of pictures of her and her parents, and a few other people. The whole place reminds me of her-sweet, warm, and inviting.

I put several cameras around her house. Yes, it's wrong. I know. I just can't seem to help myself. Surveillance is what I do. It's what I'm good at; really good. I have a burning need to protect my woman and be able to see and hear her every second of the day. I'll breathe easier just knowing that now I can see her at all times.

Serena

♥

I am on top of a ladder, putting books on the shelf, when Jax appears below. "Hey, beautiful. What are you doing?"

I smile. "Just working. How about you?"

"Just enjoying the view, sweetheart."

I have no idea what he's talking about until I see his eyes lingering on my legs. "Oh!" I must be practically flashing the man. I try to make sure I am covered while balancing on the ladder, when the Jones twins, Bruce and Bobby, race through and knock into my ladder. I fly off and brace myself for impact. Instead of hard ground, I am caught by a warm, sexy man.

"Oh my gosh! Thank you so much!" Jax continues holding me like I weigh nothing. Being in his arms is heaven. He is so solid and warm. I could stay here forever.

"Are you okay, angel?"

"Never better," I smile up at him. He smiles and lowers his head toward me when Ms. Minny interrupts us.

"Ms. Scott, you are not paid to be inappropriate with your boyfriend during library hours. Get back to work." She rounds the corner and we both burst out laughing.

"Damn. That lady is scary."

"That she is." He puts me down. I immediately miss his warmth, though his yummy scent still clings to me.

"I'd better stop being *inappropriate* and let you get back to work," he says, walking toward the door.

I laugh. "See you soon?"

He smiles. "You know it."

Ms. Minny's timing sucks! I think he would have kissed me if she hadn't interrupted. Jax has been in the library every day for the last week. I keep thinking he will ask me out, but it hasn't happened yet. He is always friendly, but he hasn't made a move.

I know that I'd never have the courage to ask him out. So how do you get a man to ask you on a date? I'm really not sure. I've never really tried to before. When you've known all the men in town your whole life, it's hard to feel romantic toward them.

Joe Briggs asked me out once, but all I could think about was when he stuck a frog down my dress when I was ten. It's silly, I know. It's just hard to have romantic feelings for someone you've literally known since you were both in diapers. No mystery. No surprises. What you see is pretty much what you get.

I hadn't been interested in anyone before, but when I saw Jax, BAM! I felt like I'd been hit over the head with a two-by-four. Obviously, he is crazy hot, but he's also really sweet. I even consider him a good friend, but I want him to be so much more. Does he feel the same? I mean, he follows me to work and back and sometimes parks across the street and watches me. That has to mean something.

I like to pretend he is completely and totally obsessed with me; watching me, stalking me. Sick, right? I even think I catch a whiff of his cologne in my house sometimes. That's how far gone I am for this man. In my imagination, he's madly, obsessively in love with me, just like I am with him.

Whenever I have a chance, I sketch him. I'm not a great artist, but I'm not too shabby. I mainly draw his face, but I also spend a lot of time drawing his naked body. Sadly, not from memory; just from imagination. I think I have filled an entire sketchbook with images of him since we met. I am clearly cuckoo.

****

That night, after a long bath, I get dressed for bed in my teeny tiny matching black lace shorts and bra top. I always feel sexy in them. I'm lying in bed, trying to come up with ideas of how to get Jax to make a move, when I spot something out of place.

Teddy, my beloved childhood teddy bear, is on the top shelf of my bookcase, as always, but he's angled. I always have him facing forward. *Always.* I take a closer look and see a tiny freaking camera on my shelf, pointed right at my bed! *What the hell?*

I give myself a few seconds to calm down. Think. Who would have done this? Who would have the opportunity? Who would know how? Who would want to? As I'm trying to come up with the answers, I hear Jax's car pulling into his driveway. All at once, it clicks. He's a security guy. I though I was imagining his scent in my house. Was he actually in here? *Holy shit!* I think Jax is full on stalking me!

You would think this discovery would terrify me, or at least send up red flags; but, no. The idea that Jax is that into me just makes my desire for him skyrocket. New plan. If he wants a show, I'll give him a show. I'm going to tempt the fuck out of my sexy stalker.

Jax

♥

I'm seriously fucked up. I spend every possible minute of my day watching Serena; thinking about all the things I want to do to my sweet angel. Don't get me wrong-I wouldn't harm a hair on her beautiful head. I just spend a lot of time imagining her puffy pink lips wrapped around my cock, swallowing my cum. I also love to picture her big tits bouncing as she rides me until I finally flip her over and fuck her so hard, she can't walk straight.

It's eleven p.m. Serena goes to bed at the same time each night. As I watch, she turns the lights off in each room before making her way to her bedroom. Yes, I put a camera there. Yes, it's wrong. Sue me.

She stretches across her bed, letting me see every tempting curve of her sexy as fuck body through the tiny pajamas she is wearing. Damn. She looks hot as hell. Just when I think that this is as bad as it's going to get, she starts running her hands all over her body and moaning. *Holy shit!*

I release my hard cock from my jeans as I watch the feed on my computer. She takes off the sleep set, revealing her firm, ripe breasts and her wet little pussy. "Oh, angel. You are killing me." She pinches her nipples, then grabs a purple vibrator from her nightstand and starts fucking her sweet cunt with it. I stroke my cock right along with her. I've never been so hard in all my life.

"Jax!" she screams as she orgasms, causing cum to gush out of my cock. *Holy shit!* I nearly black out, I come so hard. I know I'm not good enough for her, but if Serena wants me, I'm hers. I can't believe she just cried out my name as she orgasmed. The tiny shred of control I had on my desire is gone. It's time for me to claim what's mine.

Serena

♥

"Mmmm, Jax," I mumble as I feel him stroking my leg with his callused hands. "That feels so good."

I open my eyes and see Jax actually stroking my body. *Holy shit! He's really here!* "Jax?"

"Fuck. I'm sorry, Serena. I just couldn't help myself. Every time I see you, I want to touch you."

"Then touch me. Please. Mmmm," I moan as his hands stroke up my body. He touches his lips to mine, making desire rage through my body. His mouth devours mine, while his fingers pinch my nipples. I should be embarrassed, considering that I am completely naked, but I don't even care. I'm too far gone with desire to be self-conscious about my body.

I wrap my arms around him, pulling him on top of me. As he lies against me, I feel his enormous hard cock. *Wow.* He is definitely packing a lot. His jeans are all that separate his cock from my very hungry pussy. "Yessss!" I rock my hips against him, and take his shirt off.

His six pack is so sexy. I run my hands across his chest and biceps. He has a lot of tattoos and muscles. I'm sure he looks really intimidating to most people, but I just think he's sexy as hell.

He takes my mouth hungrily. He tastes like whiskey and chocolate. So delicious. I am already addicted to him. He moves down my body, kissing as he goes. He licks my pussy, causing my hips to jump off the bed. No one has ever done that to me before. I had no idea it would be so fucking amazing.

"It's okay, angel. Just relax. Let me lick up your sweet cream." He proceeds to do just that, devouring my pussy before sucking on my swollen clit, making me scream out his name as I come. He does it repeatedly, until his beard is soaked with my juices and I am boneless.

"My turn," I say, pushing him down, opening his jeans, and taking his cock in my mouth. It already has a lot of pre-cum leaking out the tip. I swirl my tongue around it, licking up every drop. "Mmmm. You taste so good, Jax. I hope I'm doing this right."

He sounds pained when he laughs. "You are doing it perfect, baby. So perfect, I'm gonna come in your mouth if you don't stop."

I suck harder, until he lets go and I feel stream after stream of his hot cum in my mouth. "Damn, angel. You are perfect."

"You, too," I say, kissing him. "Wow. That was amazing. I thought I was dreaming at first," I laugh, caressing his chest. "How did you even get in here?"

He looks away for a second. Oh, crap. He broke in here again, which I'm not supposed to know. He looks panicked. I think I just totally killed the mood. I know I should be terrified that Jax broke in here (more than once), but instead I am turned on beyond belief. I have never felt so desired.

"I'm so sorry, angel. I shouldn't have come in here while you were asleep. I'll just leave."

"No. Jax, wait! Come back!" Before I have a chance to process everything, he is gone. *Shit.*

Jax

♥

What the hell was I thinking? I wasn't. All I was focused on was making Serena mine. I wasn't thinking about how wrong that would be. I know that if I take her sweet little pussy, there will be no going back. I'll keep her forever, and be the most possessive son of a bitch you've ever seen.

I know that she deserves better; much better than a jaded ex-special forces guy twelve years her senior. She deserves a sweet kid who will treat her right; not pound into her pussy every chance they get like I dream about doing. I'd fuck every hole she has, marking her as mine. She wouldn't leave the house without my cum dripping down her thighs. I'm a fucking beast, and I know I don't deserve the perfection that is my angel.

Not to mention that I'm her fucking stalker. How do I even begin to explain that? When she realizes that I broke into her house and put in cameras, she will probably freak out. Hell, she might even call the cops. I wouldn't blame her.

She might want me now, but she would run away screaming if she knew that I watch her, follow her, jack off to her, and am completely and utterly obsessed with her. It's better this way. If she ever found out what I've done, she would be terrified of me.

Even knowing that, walking out of her bedroom was the hardest thing I've ever done. I know that even with that brief taste of her, she has ruined all other women for me. It will be her or no one; of that I am certain.

Serena

♥

What does a girl have to do to get her sexy stalker to fuck her? Jeez. I thought I would tempt Jax into making a move, and it worked, but then he freaked out. I need to do something drastic before he loses interest in me. I need to step up my game; immediately. I have a brilliant plan, and have called in reinforcements.

Jay and Sam are two very handsome men. They are good friends of mine, and a couple. Of course, Jax doesn't need to know that. I'm hoping that if he thinks he has some competition, he'll get jealous and come after me. I realize that might be a little immature, but desperate times call for desperate measures.

Jax is home. Check. Jay and Sam are on their way over. Check. I've got on a tight dress that barely covers me. Check. I take a breath. Hopefully, he is watching. Operation *seduce my stalker* is about to begin.

Jax

♥

"Who the fuck are these assholes?" I snarl. Two muscled up frat boys give Serena a hug. They let her go fairly quickly, but it's still way too long for my liking. She smiles and invites them inside. I do not like this one bit.

My angel is wearing a sexy, skintight dress that looks like something you would wear to go clubbing. Maybe she has worn sexy shit like this in front of other men before, but she won't do it again if I have any say in it. I want her sexy little body to be for my eyes only.

I keep an eye on the camera feed. The two men whistle at her as she spins around, modeling the dress for them. *Hell, no.* This is not gonna work for me. I know she deserves better, but no one else will ever love Serena like I do. It's time to go all in and stake my claim. My little angel is about to learn not to show anyone else what's mine.

Serena

"Oh, shit! I think it worked, babe. A sexy, pissed off man is headed our way," Jay whispers.

"You two are the sweetest for helping me out. I'm gonna run to the bathroom for a sec. I'll be right back." I go into the bathroom and look at myself in the mirror, taking deep breaths and trying to calm my nerves. This is it. This is my shot. Damn, I hope this works.

I hear pounding on the front door and yelling. "Leave. Now!" Jax bellows.

"Hey, man. It's all good. We're outta here," Sam says, sounding like they are moving further away. I hear the front door close.

I walk out and am immediately pushed up against the wall by my very sexy, very angry looking beast. "Jax! What are you doing here?"

"Claiming what's mine."

"It's about time," I mutter, as he picks my up, takes my mouth roughly, and pushes his body against mine.

Jax

♥

Her lips taste like cinnamon and sugar. Her mouth is a drug, and I've given up fighting my addiction. How did I think I could ever stop this obsession? I take her puffy lips over and over, getting her ready for the dirty things I plan on doing to her. I tear the sexy dress from her body, ripping it in two.

"Hey! I liked that dress!" she protests.

"Angel, I'll buy you another one. I need you naked. Now."

"Oh. Okay," she says quietly.

I take in the sight of her in a matching lacy red bra and panties. Damn. My angel is a fucking siren. "So gorgeous," I say, squeezing her plump tit. I suck her strawberry nipple into my mouth through the lace of her bra, eliciting a moan from her.

"Please don't stop, Jax. Not again."

"Oh, sweetheart. There's nothing that could stop me from taking you this time. Strip," I command. She unhooks her bra, doing a sexy little dance and trying to hide those gorgeous tits from me. She moves her hands, then pushes off her panties and kicks them aside. I take in her sexy curves and dripping wet slit.

"You look like a centerfold, baby. You are so fucking gorgeous. And you are mine. You know that, right?" I move closer, squeezing her tits, nibbling and sucking both nipples. My cock could pound nails, it's so fucking hard right now. This wisp of a woman has brought this badass to his knees.

"Yes. I am yours," she says breathlessly.

"You've been naughty, baby girl. Parading what's mine in front of those boys." I smack her round ass, making her squeak. I smack it a few more times before caressing the hurt. "That's for being naughty," I say, pushing my finger into her tight, wet heat. Oh, she liked that. She is dripping wet and writhing against me. "Who does this pussy belong to?"

"You! It belongs to you!"

"That's right, angel. From now on, this sexy as fuck body belongs to me, and only me. Do you understand?" She nods her head. "I need the words, sweetheart."

"Yes! I understand. I only want to belong to you," she pants. "Does that mean you belong to me?"

"Angel, you've owned me since the second I laid eyes on you." She smiles at that. I undo my jeans and push them down, revealing my hard cock. I pull her against me, walking as I make my way to her bedroom, holding her close and kissing her the entire way.

I lie down on the bed, pulling her on top of me, and inch inside her heat. "Fuck, angel. I'm never gonna last. I'll try to go slower next time." I slam her down on me fully, tearing through her innocence, and making her wince. *Son of a bitch.* "I'm so sorry, angel," I say, kissing her tears away. "If I'd have known, I would have gone slower."

"I wanted you out of control. I still do. It's okay," she says after a few seconds. "It doesn't hurt anymore. It actually feels amazing." I shift inside her, making her cry out. Her hot little pussy is getting used to me, and is taking me so good. "Please, Jax. Harder. Faster.

More." She cries out as she comes on my cock, choking the life out of it.

I can't deny her anything. I let go, slamming her down on my cock again and again. The wet slurping noise and tightness of her pussy are making it tough to hold on. "Come inside me, Jax," she whispers. That's all it takes for me to let go, filling her pussy with my seed.

Serena

♥

A few minutes later, Jax carries me to my bathroom. He starts a bath and has me soak in it. "Aren't you joining me?"

"I'm trying to let you recover, sweetheart."

"What if I don't want to recover? What if I want more?" I say, dragging him down and kissing him with all the hunger I feel. After the hot sex we just had, I am feeling pretty confident.

"I will give you whatever you want, baby."

"What I want is you."

"You have me already, sweetheart, but if you want me to fuck you more, that's what you'll get," he says, getting in the tub behind me.

We soak for a few minutes before he starts gently cleaning me, paying special attention to my breasts and pussy. "Jax," I whine. He rewards me by picking me up and lowering me onto his hard cock once more. "Yessss," I hiss. He helps me ride him hard, sloshing water over the sides of the tub. He slams me down on him again and again until we both come once more. He dries me off and carries me to my bed. I snuggle against his warm, solid body. If this is a dream, I never want to wake up.

Jax

♥

I watch Serena sleep. Damn, she's beautiful. I want to wake up with her every morning. That's my plan. I just need to make it happen. I guess it would be too soon to propose? Yes, probably. It would most likely scare her off. It would terrify her if she knew I bought her ring a few hours after first laying eyes on her. Yep. That's how far gone I am. One look and I knew my single days were over.

"Mmmm," she mumbles, stretching. "Oh! It wasn't a dream," she says, blinding me with her beautiful smile before kissing me seductively. "Good morning, Jax."

"Good morning, sunshine."

"You call me the sweetest things."

"That's because you are the sweetest things. You light up my world with your smile, you are the sweetest woman I've ever met, you are hot as fuck, and you make me hard as a rock."

"Hmmm. What can we do about that?" she asks, moving down my body. Before I realize what her plan is, her pouty lips are wrapped around my cock, sucking me hard.

"Damn, sweetheart. That feels so good." She takes me deeper and deeper, until I hit the back of her throat. "Angel, I'm not gonna last." She responds by sucking harder and faster. I feel tingles up my spine before my balls seize up and I explode in her mouth, coming so hard I see stars. I try to catch my breath while she licks up every drop like a good girl.

"My turn," I say, tossing her on her back. She is already soaked for me. I lick her sweetness, causing her to squirm and push my face harder against her. I stretch her with my fingers while my tongue fucks her. She gushes against my face with a scream. I eat her sweetness for several more minutes before she finally begs me to stop.

"No more. It's too much."

"Sweetheart, if you think I'm even close to done with you, you are sorely mistaken." I slam my cock to the hilt inside her. Damn. Every time, I think it can't get any better, but it does. She moans, sinking her nails into my back and pushing me deeper.

"More, Jax. Don't hold back. Fuck me hard." Her plea for me to fuck her snaps the thread of control I was holding onto. I pound into her sweet little cunt, drawing orgasm after orgasm from her.

"So fucking responsive, angel." As she comes on my cock once more, a picture of her belly round with my baby flashes through my mind, sending me into another powerful orgasm. I lie down and pull her against me, knowing I have my whole world in my arms.

Serena

♥

Jax and I have been seeing each other for a couple of weeks now. We have yet to spend a night apart. It has been perfect; almost too perfect. I keep waiting for the other shoe to drop. I know, I know. It's dumb. It's just that Jax is so wonderful, handsome, etc., and I've watched too many Lifetime movies. I keep worrying that he'll turn out to be a serial killer, or have a secret family stashed somewhere. I really don't worry about these crazy scenarios when we are together. But when I'm alone (though it has not been often; believe me), my imagination runs wild.

I try to put my negative thoughts aside as the doorbell rings. Jax is here to take me to the Fall Festival. I open the door, once again stunned by how ridiculously sexy this man is. He steps forward, giving me a kiss. "Damn, babe. You look gorgeous."

I look down at myself. I'm wearing my favorite jeans and a snug sweater. They fit me well. "You don't look so bad yourself, handsome." I stand on my tiptoes to kiss him again.

After a few minutes, he pulls away. "Angel, unless you want to spend all day in bed, we need to leave."

"That doesn't sound so bad," I pout, "but I suppose I can wait a few hours." He growls and grabs my ass as I race past him.

Jax

♥

The Fall Festival is impressive, to say the least. I feel like I'm in a fucking Hallmark movie. There is a giant pumpkin patch, hay maze, haunted barn, s'mores, hot dogs, face painting, pumpkin carving, and more. Children race around, screaming and laughing. I didn't know places like this existed in real life.

"This would be a great place to raise a family," I mention casually.

"I agree!" Serena smiles blindingly at me.

I lean down to whisper in her ear. "You do realize that I'm doing my damnedest to knock you up, sweetheart." Her mouth drops open in shock. I put my finger under her chin to close it. "I love you, baby," I say, kissing her tenderly.

"Oh, Jax," she smiles tearfully, "I love you, too. It's been so hard not to tell you. I didn't want you to think I was rushing you."

"Angel, believe me, this can't move fast enough for me." The day is perfect. We spend a few hours walking around, enjoying the festival. I learn that Serena loves s'mores and pumpkin seeds, and hates pumpkin pie. We talk a lot, getting to know each other even better.

I tell her about my parents, who died a few years back. They had me late in life. I was a miracle baby; an only child, just like her. They loved me fiercely. I was devastated to lose them. That was when my Army buddies became my only family.

I share things with her I have never shared with anyone. I fall deeper and deeper in love with her every day. Everything is absolutely perfect. I just hope this bubble of happiness doesn't burst.

Serena

♥

This is the first time I've been in Jax's house since he moved in. For whatever reason, we always stay at my house. I wander around the living room and kitchen while he cooks, taking everything in. He hasn't done much decorating, but that's not too surprising. After all, he hasn't been here for very long, and I keep him pretty busy.

"The food smells delicious, Jax." I'm not joking. The scent of garlic and cheese is making my mouth water.

"I'm not a master chef, sunshine, but I do make a mean pasta," he smiles before coming over to kiss me. "Almost done." I help him plate everything, and we sit down to our first home-cooked meal together.

"Oh my God. This is amazing!" Seriously, all pasta is good, but this is beyond.

"I'm glad you like it."

We eat dinner while talking nonstop. He tells me a lot more about his security work. The good news is that most of his work is done on his computer, so he pretty much works from home, though he does go in to the office for a meeting with his partners at least once a week.

After cleaning up the kitchen, we settle down on his couch to watch a reality dating show. We both make fun of it because it is so freaking ridiculous. These people are so full of drama!

I am warm and comfy snuggling against him. After awhile, my eyes feel so heavy. I nod off on the couch, waking briefly to him undressing me and tucking me into his bed. "Go back to sleep, angel," he says, kissing me softly.

"Goodnight," I murmur, before sacking out again.

Serena

♥

I wake up snuggled against Jax. Every day with him is awesome. Sometimes I feel like he's holding something back, but it's probably just my imagination. I've never been in a relationship before, so what do I know?

I think about waking him with a blow job, because it is a great morning ritual for both of us, but realize he might actually need some sleep. He spends so much time taking care of me, I'm not sure he's getting enough rest. I decide that I'll make us a fabulous breakfast. After all, it is Sunday. We have all day.

After some time, I have some homemade cinnamon rolls ready, along with eggs and bacon. I've made enough to feed an army. I'm about to go wake Jax when a door by the kitchen creaks open. I assume it is a pantry that I hadn't noticed. When I peak inside, what I find stuns me.

Pictures of me; like hundreds. They cover every surface of the closet. I mean, I did kind of know he was stalking me, but this is so far beyond that. This is not normal behavior. There are so many pictures, along with some of my underwear. "What the fuck?"

Jax

♥

I wake up alone. Surely she didn't leave. I will spank her sexy little ass. I hear clanging, and realize she is making us breakfast. What a woman!

I take a quick piss, then head in the other room to find her. "What the fuck?" I hear her say.

"What's wrong, babe?" I walk in the room and come to a screeching halt as I see her peering into my hidden room. "Oh, shit. Let me explain." Oh, God. This isn't good. "Okay. I know it looks like I'm some obsessed psycho, but I swear I'm not; not a psycho, I mean. I am obsessed with you, but in a good way. I've been in love with you since I first set eyes on you. I found a house close to yours. I've followed you, watched you, jacked off to you. Angel, you are everything to me. I would never hurt you, though. Never. You are my obsession. I want to be with you all the time. I love you so much."

She looks at me for several seconds before turning back to the closet; the one that is a fucking shrine to her. She spends several minutes looking it over. "This is...wow. I don't know what to say. Have you ever done this to anyone else?" she asks, narrowing her eyes with what looks like jealousy.

"No. I swear. I have never done this to another woman. I have never wanted another woman like I want you. I have never loved another woman." I take her hands and make sure she sees the sincerity in my eyes. "I'm sure you can't understand my obsession, but I can't help myself. You are all that I think about every second of the day."

She looks at me and smiles. "I understand better than you think," she grabs her knapsack and starts rifling through it, pulling out a notebook. "Here," she thrusts it at me. "Look through this."

"What is this?" I open the notebook up and see a damn good drawing of me. "Wow. That's really good."

"Thanks. Keep going." I do, finding page after page of sketches of me. There are even some of me holding my cock in my hand.

"Angel, these are great, but I have to say, I'm a little offended at the size of my dick in your drawings."

She laughs. "Well, that was before I had seen you naked. I was just using my imagination. I will go back and make corrections now that I know what you actually look like."

I flip through more, finding sketches of the two of us getting married, having a baby, and Mrs. Jaxon Stone written all over. "What does all of this mean, sunshine?"

She puts her arms around me. "It means that I am obsessed with you, too, sexy stalker."

"Thank God!" I pull her close for a kiss. "I really thought I had screwed things up with you for good."

"No, Jax. But from now on, no secrets. Okay?"

"Anything for you, angel. So, if you are obsessed, too, does it mean it's not too soon for a proposal?"

"Are you serious?" she asks as I race to the other room to get the engagement ring I bought for her. I kneel down in front of her.

"My angel. I have been in love with you since I first saw you. I am obsessed with you, probably to an unhealthy degree. I love you so much. All I want to do is marry you and put my babies in you. Will you marry me?"

"Yes!" she says, wiping tears away. "I love you, too, you crazy man. I will marry you. Just how many babies are we planning on?"

"That's up to you, angel. I will do my damnedest to keep you knocked up, starting now."

Serena

♥

*T*wo weeks later...

When Jax facetimed my parents after he proposed, I thought he was nuts. They were stunned, to say the least; my dad especially. He started telling us that we couldn't know that we were in love so quickly. When I reminded him that he proposed to Mom on sight and married her three days later, he backed off a bit.

That was two weeks ago. My parents got home yesterday. Things were a little tense at first, but they really like Jax. They could see how much we love each other.

Right now, Mom is helping me into a gorgeous, sparkly wedding dress. I feel like a princess. "Oh, honey! You look so beautiful!" she says, wiping away her tears.

"Thank you, but please stop crying! You are going to make me ruin my makeup." We both laugh.

Emily and Savannah run through the door, giggling. "There are a lot of seriously hot men at your wedding! Just saying. Oh, Serena, you look gorgeous!"

Both of my friends tear up. "Stop it! Both of you! No crying!"

My dad knocks, then pokes his head inside. "Your man is looking pretty darn impatient up there. You girls might need to get a move on before he drags you down the aisle."

We all laugh, but I wouldn't put it past him, so we hurry it up.

Jax

♥

"Calm down, man. What is with this town? I've never seen so many grown ass men so eager to get married," says Slade.

"Just wait until you find your woman."

The music starts playing. Two of Serena's friends walk down the aisle first. When she walks in, I am stunned speechless. She is the most beautiful thing I have ever seen. I can't wait to make her my wife.

Her father walks her to me. "Angel, you look stunning," I say, kissing her lips gently.

"Thank you. You do, too."

"Let's get this show on the road so I can take you home and have my wicked way with you."

"Looking forward to it, sexy stalker."

Jax

♥

I carry my beautiful bride across the threshold of our house. Something about knowing she is my wife is making me really emotional. It is also turning me into a caveman that wants to claim her and show the world that she is mine.

I carry her upstairs to our bedroom. I had her friends pretty it up with rose petals and lights. "Oh, Jax. This is so gorgeous!" she says, tearing up.

"I'll take you wherever you want to go for a belated honeymoon in a few months when you have time off. I couldn't wait any longer to wife you up, though."

"Well, we probably shouldn't wait too long, or we won't be able to go," she says coyly.

"Why wouldn't we be able to go, sunshine?"

"I think that once you are too far along in your pregnancy, they won't let you fly."

I'm stunned speechless. "Are you saying...?" I manage to get out. My voice is rough with emotion.

"Yep. You have already managed to knock me up."

I pick her up and hold her against me. "You're damn right I did! Angel, you have made me the happiest man in the world. "I love you so much."

"I love you, too," she smiles her siren smile. She takes off her dress to reveal the sexiest fucking bridal lingerie I've ever seen. My cock turns to stone instantly. "Well, husband, what ever are you going to do with me now that I'm yours?"

"Whatever I want, my sweet wife. Whatever I want."

We spend hours enjoying each other before nodding off to a deep, peaceful sleep.

Epilogue–Serena

♥

Ten years later...

I lock the front door to the library and turn off the lights in each area. A loud noise makes me jump. "Is someone there?" Strong arms clamp around me, pulling me against a hard, muscular body. "Please don't hurt me," I whisper as I feel wetness pool between my legs.

The man slides his palms across my nipples, pinching each one. "Angel, the only thing I'm gonna do to you is fuck you so hard, you may never recover."

"Yes. Please," I hum as he strokes my sides before pulling up my dress.

"Damn, baby. You don't have any panties on. If I'd have known that, I wouldn't have been able to wait until you closed up. Someone could have seen your sweet pussy. I think this deserves a punishment," he says, delivering two hard smacks against my bare ass.

"Ouch!" I cry out, then moan as he starts rubbing away the pain.

"Does that feel good, baby?"

"Oh yes, sexy stalker, but I have other places that hurt, too."

"Hmmm. Now where would that be? Here?" he says, pushing his fingers into my dripping heat.

"Yes! I feel so empty. I need something big and hard to fill me up."

"Sweetheart, I've got just what you need," he says, freeing his huge cock from his pants. With no preamble, he pushes me down on my desk and slams all the way in. Our role play is usually drawn out a little more, but sometimes, like tonight, we are far too desperate for each other to go slow.

You can't see us from outside, and the security feed is only watched by my sexy man, so I'm not too worried about anyone seeing us. This happens at least a few times a week, along with him stalking me; driving me insane with desire.

Even after being with him for so long, his big cock stretches me so wide every time. Nothing else in the world has ever felt as good as when he fucks me. "Fuck! Jax, that feels so good!"

"Fuck, baby. Your tight little pussy is strangling my cock. I'm not gonna last long. I need you to come hard and milk my big cock with that sweet little cunt of yours."

"Jax!" I scream as I come hard, clawing his back. "Come inside me," I say as my pussy squeezes him tight. He slams inside me a few more times before groaning my name. He explodes, dripping cum down my legs, then collapsing on top of me. "Ummm. That was so good."

"It always is, angel."

He holds me for a few minutes before we get up from the very hard, uncomfortable desk and get dressed, stopping every few seconds to kiss. Thank God Ms. Minny isn't here anymore. She would have a coronary if she knew that we had sex (frequently!) in the library. Talk about inappropriate behavior! She retired several years ago and moved to Florida, leaving me as the head librarian.

There are papers strewn everywhere, but I don't care. All I care about is being with my sexy husband. He looks just as gorgeous as ever. He has a few more lines on his face and is a silver fox now. We are still just as obsessed with each other as we were when we first got together. I love this man so much, and I know he loves me, too. I let him stalk me fairly often. We both enjoy it a lot.

He starts piling all the papers back on my desk. I giggle. It's a mess, but I'll deal with it tomorrow. Right now, we have to get home to our three kids.

"I'm taking you to dinner tonight."

"Jax, we can't keep Mom on babysitting duty for that long. She's been there all day."

"Your mom lives to be with her grand babies. Besides, she offered to watch them a little longer so we could have some alone time," he says, kissing the back of my neck.

"Adults only time with my sexy stalker husband? Count me in!"

We close the library, walking out the door hand in hand. We are so happy with each other and our little family. Being with each other makes us both feel complete in a way we weren't before. We make each other better. We are every bit as in love and obsessed with each other as we were all those years ago; maybe even more so.

Jax takes me in his arms, kissing me hard. "Mmm. What was that for?"

"I just want you to know how much I love you."

"I love you, too. More than anything."

Who would have thought that my handsome stalker and I would have such a sweet and sexy happily ever after?

THE END

Seducing Shelly

Lacy Jane

Lacy Jane Publishing

Contents

Shelly

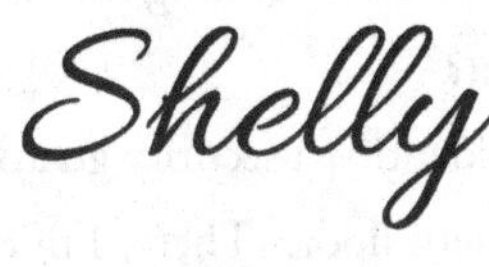

"**I**'m freaking out!" I say, pacing back and forth on the sidewalk.

"You'll be fine," my bestie, Ella, reassures me over the phone. "You'll kick ass and take names! You are a force to be reckoned with. You've got this. Now, go get 'em!"

"Okay. I will. Thanks. Love you."

"Love you, too. Good luck!"

I hang up and look at the massive high rise in front of me; Sterling Enterprises. Yep. Not intimidating at all. It's only one of the biggest companies in the country; sitting at the top of the Fortune 500 list, alongside Apple and Walmart.

This position comes with a great salary, profit sharing, health insurance, and a ton of vacation time; not to mention, a lot of upward mobility. They frequently promote from within. I just have to get my foot in the door. I take a deep breath and square my shoulders. *I will get this job. I will get this job.* I repeat the mantra in my head. Power of positive thinking and all that, you know.

I just graduated from business school at the top of my class, and managed to land an interview at Sterling-my dream company. Not too shabby for a twenty-one year old. I would be starting out as an assistant, but that is fine with me. I have no problem working my way up the corporate ladder before running the company one day. A girl needs goals. Am I right?

After verifying my identity, a security guard directs me to take an elevator up to the fiftieth floor. There, I'm escorted through a set of heavy glass doors to meet Anne Winters; the head of HR and the person who will determine my fate.

She's an attractive, middle-aged brunette who looks like she was probably a model at one time. She towers over me, but then who doesn't? As we talk, I begin to relax. She is actually quite nice and not as intimidating as I would have expected. I could even see us being friends.

As we conclude the meeting, she turns to me, smiling. "Well, if you want the job, it's yours."

"Oh my gosh! Thank you so much! You won't regret it!" I say, impulsively giving her a hug. She laughs and starts gathering a ton of paperwork for me to fill out before I start on Monday. The door suddenly flies open, startling me, and time stands still.

There is an incredibly hot man standing there. I mean, seriously hot. Drench your panties and harden your nipples hot. That's what happens to me, anyway. He's well over six feet of muscle packed into a beautiful gray suit that struggles to contain his giant biceps, and his large, sexy frame takes up most of the doorway. Yum.

He's got gorgeous, silky black hair, and a five o' clock shadow that I long to touch. *I bet it's really soft. What would it feel like between my legs? Would it scratch my thighs? What would it feel like stroking my clit? Oh my gosh! Stop the naughty thoughts!*

I finally reach his emerald eyes. I've been so busy staring at him, I didn't realize he was returning the favor. My tummy flutters as his eyes rake over me, setting me on fire. My breath catches. He is quite a bit older than me, but *damn*, does he look good!

Finally, he speaks in a gravelly voice that sends shivers up and down my spine. "Sorry, Anne. I didn't know you were with someone. I'll catch up with you later." With that, he turns, giving me an incredible view of his muscular back and rock hard ass. Once he leaves, I am finally able to think clearly again.

"Wow. That man is *seriously* hot. Who is he?"

Anne seems amused. She mumbles what sounds like "this is going to be fun," before grinning at me and saying, "That, my dear, is your new boss, Jeremy Strong. Surprise!"

Holy shit! I am so fucked.

Jeremy

♥

When I open the door to Anne's office, I don't expect to see an angel in the flesh. A tiny little thing with strawberry blonde hair and unusual amber eyes. She is short, but has a ton of curves packed on her little body.

I am rendered speechless at the sight of her. It takes several seconds before I can think clearly enough to say something and leave. Thank God my jacket covers the instant hard-on I had the moment I laid eyes on her. I sit at my desk, trying to concentrate, but all I can think about is the woman with the amber eyes and sultry pink lips, and all the depraved things I'd like to do to her.

A short time later, Anne walks in to see what I wanted. After we spend a few minutes discussing business, I ask the question I'm dying to know the answer to. "So, who was the woman in your office?" I ask casually.

She chuckles. "I wondered how long it would take you to ask. That is Shelly; your new assistant. She starts Monday."

Well, shit. I finally find the woman of my dreams, and she is off limits to me. As it is, my cock is hard enough to pound nails. What will it be like being around her every day? I've never been remotely tempted by anyone working for me before, but then again, none of them were Shelly. *I am so fucked.*

Shelly

♥

I show up bright and early for my first day of work. I am very excited to be here and want to make a good first impression. Also, I must admit, I am dying to see Jeremy Strong again. Hopefully, he isn't as scorching hot as I remember, or my brain will turn to mush around him.

As soon as I walk in, I realize that he's not as hot as I remember him being; he's even hotter. Good lord. I feel bad for the rest of the male population. Looks, smarts, power; he's got it all. How does any woman work for him and get anything done? I could spend all day just looking at him; that's how gorgeous he is. I'll just have to fake it till I make it, and try not to jump on his incredibly sexy body.

He's sitting at his desk, so I knock lightly on the door and walk in. "Hi, Mr. Strong. I'm Shelly, your new assistant," I say, holding out my hand.

He clasps it firmly in his. Just that innocent touch sends electricity directly to my pussy, drenching my panties. My nipples instantly pebble, and I have an unbearable ache between my legs. Am I ever in trouble.

"Very nice to meet you, Shelly," he says in his deep, sexy voice. Goosebumps break out on my arms. It's hard to even think straight in his presence. How am I ever going to behave myself with this man?

He gives me a list of things I need to get done. I spend my time at work concentrating on my tasks, and doing my best to ignore him and my body's reaction to him. This becomes my strategy over the next month. It's the only way I know of to cope with this overwhelming attraction I feel toward my boss.

Jeremy

♥

How am I ever going to behave myself with this woman? I've already jacked myself off in the bathroom three times today alone just thinking about her. Not that it helped. No, nothing will help except driving my cock deep inside this beautiful woman until we both pass out from exhaustion.

She purses her lips, and bites the end of her pencil. Just like that, my mind is right back in the gutter, imagining better uses for that sexy mouth of hers. *Those puffy lips would open wide for my big cock. She would suck and lick my cockhead like a lollipop. Then I would fuck her throat until she gagged, but she would love every second of it, getting herself off along with me. When I finally explode in her mouth, she would gladly swallow down every drop of cum like the good girl she is.*

And just like that, I'm hard as a fucking rock again. I'm resigned to my fate. As long as she works for me, this will be my life; a hard cock all day long, every day, with no end in sight. Can a man die of blue balls? It sure as hell feels like it.

Damn! Does she have to bend over like that to get those files? Fuck! Her full, heart shaped ass is in the air. It takes every ounce of my willpower not to push her down and fuck her like she's never been fucked before.

I'm her boss. Hitting on her would be abuse of power at best; sexual harassment at worst. I can't do anything about this unrelenting pull I feel toward her. Maybe I'll get used to her, and won't find her so irresistible after we've spent more time together. This attraction will get easier to resist, right? I sure as hell hope so. As it is, I feel like a starving animal eyeing a steak dinner. She is everything I've ever wanted, wrapped in a delicious, curvy little package.

Jeremy

♥

In case you were wondering, no, it hasn't gotten easier. In fact, the last month has been fucking excruciating. Everything about Shelly does it for me. Her bright smile beams sunlight into my day, her sweet floral scent immediately turns my cock to stone, and her curvy little figure (poured into various dresses designed to torture me) makes it impossible for me to concentrate on anything but her.

She is driving me fucking insane. Nothing can happen. I can't hit on her. I'm her boss, for God's sake. Plus, I am twelve years older than her. She probably thinks of me as an old man. She could have any man she wanted just by batting her long, dark, eyelashes at them. What makes me think she would want to settle for me?

After a light knock, the object of my obsession enters my office wearing a tight black skirt that looks painted on, showcasing her generous curves to the fullest. Her blouse has the first two buttons undone, showing a hint of her heavy breasts.

She bends down to file some papers, shooting that sexy little ass in the air again. Only this time, her short skirt inches up, revealing a scrap of black lace that barely covers her gorgeous ass. *Fuuuck!!!*

I don't even realize I've groaned out loud until she turns around, probably catching me staring. "What's wrong, Mr. Strong?"

How do I answer that? *Your sexy little ass is about to drive me to the breaking point. My cock is so fucking hard, it could drive nails. I need to destroy that sweet little pussy and ruin you for any other man. I want to tie you to my bed and fuck you until neither of us can think straight.* I finally settle for, "Nothing. I just have a headache." It's true enough. Lack of sleep and sexual frustration will do that to a man.

"Here, Mr. Strong. Let me help. My mom gets migraines, and this always helps her," she says as she stops right in front of me. Her generous tits are mere inches from my face, just longing to be touched and sucked. She leans closer and starts massaging my temples and the top of my head. I let out a moan of pleasure. Her hands are magical.

"That feels so good, baby. Don't stop." *Shit.* I didn't mean to call her baby. She probably thinks I'm a dirty old man now. I'm sure she doesn't mean for this massage to be anything other than pain relief.

Instead of acting offended like I expect her to, she comes even closer, pushing her breasts into my face as she massages my head. Damn it. I'm not a saint. I can't resist any longer. I put my hands on her hips, and start stroking up and down slowly. I'm trying to contain the animal in me, but it is almost impossible with her so close. "Shelly? Do you want something to happen between us?"

"Yes," she whispers. I look up into her beautiful eyes and see burning desire. I stand up, grab the back of her head and slam my mouth against hers; giving in to all of the hunger I've been holding back for the last month.

"Jeremy, yes," she moans against my mouth. I take her mouth again and again, fucking it with my teeth and tongue. She tastes so fucking sweet; even better than I've imagined. I look her in the eyes as I slowly unbutton her blouse, squeezing her full breasts and sucking her hard nipples through the rough, black lace. "Oh my god!" Her nails dig into my back, dragging me closer.

I lay her down on my desk, and spend several minutes licking and kissing her stomach, tits, and neck. I hike up her tight skirt, and move her panties aside to feel her little soaked slit.

We both moan. "Baby, you are fucking drenched for me." I push two fingers inside and start fucking her with them. Damn, she's tight. Even with as wet as she is, I can barely fit them in there.

I sit back down in my chair, pulling her pussy against my mouth. I lick and suck, groaning at how good she tastes. I'm already addicted to her sweet little cunt. I can't wait to eat it every day. "Damn, baby. You taste so good."

I fuck her hard with my tongue and fingers. The sound of her wetness and moans fills the quiet room, turning me on even more. I suck her swollen little clit into my mouth, making her scream and come all over my face. I feel a gush of wetness coat my beard. I lick up every drop, and come hard in my pants like a schoolboy.

I clean us both up, and we stare at each other for several seconds, breathing hard, before a loud knock sounds against the door. "Shit!" Shelly whisper yells while straightening her clothes and buttoning her blouse. I try to help her, but I'm all thumbs.

"Just a second!" I shout. A few moments later, my boss and friend, Prince Sterling, barges into my office. Although I hope we both look presentable, I can tell by the smirk on my boss's face that he knows exactly what's going on. Shelly races back to her desk, without saying a word.

"Care to tell me what's going on?"

Jeremy

♥

I clear my throat, deciding exactly what I want to say. Prince is one of my oldest and best friends, but he's also my boss. I'm not sure how much I should tell him. "It's not a big deal, Jeremy."

"What are you talking about?"

"That you are involved with your assistant."

"But it's against the rules..."

"No, it's really not."

"What are you talking about? I assumed there was a policy against dating coworkers."

"Well, not that I know of, and it *is* my company. The two of you just need to sign off on some papers with HR saying that you are in a consensual relationship."

"That's it?"

"That's it. Well, that and try not to attack the poor girl during business hours. What's the problem?"

I hesitate for a moment. I feel so relieved that I can finally have Shelly without consequences, but I'm suddenly full of insecurities. I take a breath. "She's a total knockout, she's smart, and she's really fucking young. She's got her whole life ahead of her, and could have anyone she wants. What would she want with an old guy like me?"

"Jesus.　You make it sound like you're ninety.　You're only thirty-three.　You aren't that much older, and you've always had more than your fair share of female attention.　Hell, you were on the "most eligible bachelor" list with me.　You're rich as hell; not as rich as me, but who is?" He grins. "Besides, she obviously returns your interest or she wouldn't have been in here with you."

"You think so?" I ask eagerly.

He rolls his eyes.　"Look. I don't need to know the details, but her blouse was buttoned wrong, her lips were puffy, and her hair was messed up.　She looked loved up.　She didn't exactly look like she was being forced to do anything against her will."

I smile. "So you think this is okay?"

"Yeah, buddy.　I think it will be fine. Just lock the damn door next time.　Now, let me tell you about the ridiculous ball that my mother has cooked up..."

Shelly

Oh my God! I cannot believe Jeremy Strong just gave me the hottest orgasm of my life. After constantly fantasizing about him, I'm stunned to find out that he is actually interested in me; like *really* interested in me, if how hard his cock was is anything to go by. That was far and away the best kiss I've ever had, and (by a landslide) the best orgasm. Not to mention, the only one ever given to me by someone besides myself.

If Mr. Sterling hadn't walked in on us, I think my boss would have fucked me right on top of his desk, and I would have gladly let him. I've never been so turned on in my life. I had no idea anyone could make me feel so good.

How is he going to act toward me now? Will he be a ravenous beast like he was earlier, or will he go back to the straight as an arrow boss that I'm used to seeing each and every day?

Unfortunately, he and Mr. Sterling have to leave for a meeting, and I don't see him for the rest of the day. Damn! I was really hoping we could pick up where we left off. Was this a one time thing? I certainly hope not. If so, it would break my heart. I'm already that far gone for my boss.

The reality of Jeremy is even better than the fantasy. I end up spending a very long and sleepless night tossing and turning; imagining what would have happened if we hadn't been interrupted.

He rips my panties off, then shoves his tongue in me again. "Oh my god! Don't stop!"

"Don't worry, baby. Nothing can stop me from claiming this sweet little pussy. You are mine!" He licks and sucks, pumping in and out of me with two fingers. It feels so good, but I need more. He sucks hard on my clit, making me scream and gush all over his face, just like before.

He pulls me closer, grinding his cock against me through his clothes. I come again just from the pressure of his hardness against my clit. I look up dazedly to see him shoving his pants down. His giant cock is hard as a rock, and already leaking precum. Without hesitation, he slams every inch of it inside me, making me arch off the desk. He fucks me harder and harder, making me scream until I'm hoarse. He then wraps my knees around his shoulders, spreading me wide, and taking me hard and rough, just like I want him to. His cock hits my clit with every thrust. He feels so good. He's going to make me come again.

"That's it, baby. Come all over my cock."

Beep! Beep! Beep! My alarm wakes me from the hottest dream I've ever had, leaving me on the verge of an orgasm. There's no way I can get through my day being this riled up. I push my fingers inside my pussy, finding it soaked. I picture my sexy boss thrusting his thick cock inside me, and orgasm almost immediately, drenching my sheets.

It feels good, believe me, but I want the real thing. I'm like an addict; one taste of him and I'm already hooked. I don't care that he's my boss. I need him inside me asap.

Shelly

I didn't hear from Jeremy yesterday after I left the office. I don't know what I expected. I guess I just hoped that he would text or call to say he was thinking about me. Nothing. Crickets.

I've taken extra care in my appearance today, styling my hair into bouncy waves, and wearing a retro pin-up girl dress. It emphasizes my assets. Hopefully my sexy boss will notice.

When he walks into the office, my breath catches in my throat. I've never seen him like this. He's not holding anything back. He looks like he wants to eat me alive. His emerald eyes rake over me, taking in my outfit. As I look him over, my eyes zero in on the hard bulge pressing against his slacks. Ooh. Glad to see my efforts aren't in vain.

We stand there staring at each other, when an attractive older woman walks in. "Shit," Jeremy says under his breath. "Hi, Mom."

"Hello, darling!" she enthuses, hugging him, before turning to me. "I'm Gina, Jeremy's mom. It's so very nice to meet you, dear."

"Hi, Gina. I'm Shelly. It's nice to meet you, too," I say nervously.

"I've heard a lot about you and just wanted to stop by and meet you since I was in the neighborhood. I'll see you both soon." She stuns me by giving me a hug on her way out.

"What was that all about?" I ask.

"That, my dear, was my mother being nosy. Someone must have mentioned our relationship to her, and she wanted to come see you for herself. The idea that her son might not be an eternal bachelor has apparently gotten her all excited."

"Oh," I blush. "She seems very nice."

"She is. I love my mother dearly, but she does like to poke her nose in my business sometimes. Speaking of business, I need you to go to HR. They have some papers for you to fill out."

"Are you firing me?" I ask; stunned beyond belief that he would do something like that.

"Good lord, no. We just need to do this by the book so that neither of our jobs are affected. There is some paperwork stating that we are in a consensual relationship. I've already filled mine out."

"Oh. Okay." I smile up at him. "So, this is really happening?"

"Yes, baby. It is definitely happening." He gives me a long kiss, then pats my butt.

"Once you do that, you can go ahead and go home for the day. I'll be out of the office in meetings all day, anyway. Sterling Enterprises is having a ball tomorrow. Apparently, Prince's mother is trying to find a wife for him. I want you to go with me as my date."

"Really?"

"Of course. I'll pick you up at seven tomorrow night."

Anne grins wide at me as I take the paperwork from her. "I never thought I'd see the day. So many women have tried and failed to land Mr. Sterling. Then you come in and he's a goner the second he lays eyes on you. I do love a good romance!"

We spend a few minutes laughing and talking. After filling out my paperwork, I leave work with a definite pep in my step, and call my best friend, Ella.

"Hey, Shelly. What's up?"

"You are not going to believe this. The Sterling family is having a full on ball at their estate this Saturday, and we are going!"

She laughs. "Why on earth would we go to a ball?"

"Do you remember me telling you about Jeremy Strong?"

"Hmmm. Let me think...oh, yeah. The man that you've been obsessed with since you first saw him when you interviewed at Sterling Enterprises last month? That guy? Now that he's your boss, you probably only mention him twenty or thirty times a day."

"Okay. So, I might be crushing on him just a teeny bit. Anyway, he is going, and he wants me to go with him! I know it's a work thing, but maybe I can finally get his attention and it can be more. I had him put you on the guest list, too. We will have to have a girl's day on Saturday to get ready for it; hair, nails, ball gowns. I'm picking you up first thing Saturday morning!"

She laughs. "Okay. It sounds like I don't have a choice."

"Nope. You don't. I'll see you bright and early Saturday. We can drop Cujo off with Mom, then spend the day getting beautiful." Cujo is Ella's little guard dog. No matter how nice I am to that little shit, he merely tolerates me. Same with my mom. The only person he actually likes is Ella. He's all about her. Mom or I always watch him if Ella goes anywhere, though, because she lives with her stepmom, and that lady is a bitch with a capital B. Anyway, that's a story for another time.

I hang up with Ella and realize I am beyond excited about tomorrow. I feel bad that I haven't told her everything that has happened with Jeremy, but I don't want to jinx it until we are officially a couple.

Jeremy

♥

"Hello, Mom. I wondered how long it would take me to hear from you."

"Oh, darling. I love Shelly already. She is adorable! When will you bring her to the house? When will I have grandchildren?"

I laugh. "Mom, you are getting way ahead of yourself. Please don't scare her off. Yes, I am crazy about her, but this is very new."

"Okay. Just make sure I'm invited to the wedding."

"Of course. Now, I have to go so I can make arrangements for the ball this weekend."

"Okay, darling. Just don't mess up, or someone else will snatch that girl up."

"Don't worry. I intend to make this official as soon as possible."

As I hang up with my mother, I realize that I am all in. I am ready for everything with Shelly. The idea of children, which used to terrify me, now sounds incredibly appealing. I am ready to wife her up and put a baby in her as soon as possible. I am already madly in love with her. I just hope she feels the same about me.

Shelly

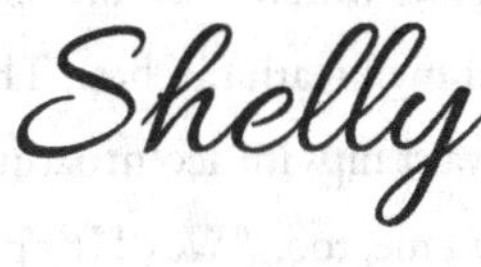

Ella and I have been best friends since kindergarten when I introduced myself and told her we were now besties. I had decided that she seemed nice and would be the perfect friend for me. I tend to speak my mind and can sometimes be a little on the pushy side.. Anyway, thankfully she agreed, and we've been inseparable ever since. We were both high IQ kids who graduated high school early together, then finished college early, too. Despite her living in a freaking castle, we have always had a lot in common.

We start our day of beauty off with mani-pedis. We talk through the manicures, laughing hysterically. The manicurists keep glaring at us. *Damn.* Loosen up a bit already. These bitches apparently do not love their jobs. Even though they aren't a ton of fun, our nails do look fab when they are finished.

The dress search isn't easy. I need something to knock Jeremy on his ass, but I haven't found it yet. By early afternoon, we have gone to three stores and struck out at each one.

Our last stop is *Your Fairy Godmother's*. When we walk in, I finally feel optimistic about finding a fabulous dress. There are gorgeous dresses as far as the eye can see. My eyes land on a stunning pink confection.

"Oh my gosh, El! This is it!" I touch the luscious tulle dress that shimmers as it moves. I race with it to the dressing room. After pulling it on, I take a look and my breath catches. The bodice clings to my large breasts, and the waist nips in; accentuating my hourglass figure. The color looks great on me, too. "Wow! It's perfect!" I exclaim.

"Well, let's see it." I practically float out of the dressing room to show my dreamy dress to Ella. "Wow! You look gorgeous! Jeremy won't know what hit him."

"From your lips to God's ears."

Ella quickly finds a great dress, too. It's a gorgeous blue color that changes as it moves. She looks stunning. I grab a tiara and put it on her head. "Ta-da!"

"Perfect! You look every inch a princess!" enthuses an adorable little old lady. "I'm Nan, the owner. You can just call me your fairy godmother. Your prince won't know what hit him."

Ella laughs. "I don't have a prince, but thank you." We happily pay for our purchases, then leave to get our hair and makeup done. Finally, we go to my place to finish getting ready for the ball. I have never been so nervous in all my life.

Jeremy

♥

The limo pulls up in front of Shelly's to pick her up. I'm as nervous as a teenager on his first date. It's been years since I've been with anyone, and even longer since I've had any kind of romantic relationship. It never seemed worth the hassle; until her.

I knock loudly. Even though I know she will be dressed to the nines, the sight of Shelly in her ball gown sucks all the air from my lungs. She's the most beautiful thing I've ever seen. I manage to get out, "Damn, you look beautiful, Shelly."

"Thank you. You look very handsome," she says, smiling up at me.

I introduce myself to Ella, who is Shelly's best friend. She seems really sweet, and is very pretty, too. I'm so obsessed with Shelly, though, that other women have pretty much ceased to exist for me. I can't take my eyes off her.

I escort the girls to the limo. I keep my hand on Shelly's back, barely resisting the urge to go lower. I sit next to her, staring unapologetically at the vision she makes. She looks like a beautiful princess in a fairy tale. I push my hand under her dress and up her leg a bit. If we were alone, I would skip this ball and take her home with me, where I would spend the night showing her that she is mine. Unfortunately, we aren't alone, so all I can do is touch her and gaze upon her beauty, while I think of all of the depraved things I'm going to do to her when I get her alone.

I nibble on her neck, pressing kisses against it. Goosebumps break out on her skin. "You look beautiful in this dress, baby girl," I whisper against her ear. "You'll look even better once I have you out of it." A dark blush covers her face.

We soon pull up in front of the Sterling mansion. I help the girls out of the limo. I finally have a date with the woman of my dreams. I won't do anything to blow it. By the end of the night, Shelly will know for certain that she belongs to me.

All I can say is wow. As hot as Jeremy looks every day in his suits, a tux just takes it up a few notches. He looks like James Bond; a super hot, really fuckable James Bond.

In the limo, he kept moving his hand up my leg, turning me on beyond belief. I have no doubt that if Ella hadn't been with us, he would be inside me right this second. If we weren't expected by the Sterlings, I would be perfectly happy to stay in the limo with him, and see what happens.

I have no bra on since my dress is backless. I hope he can't see how pebbled my nipples are from his attention. His hand never leaves my back, making my skin heat with desire. I'm looking forward to this ball, but I'm even more excited about afterward.

While we walk down the massive staircase, he never takes his eyes off me. It makes me uncomfortable, but in a good way. How I have attracted his attention, I don't know, but I am so happy to have it. He takes my hand and tugs me down a hallway. "Where are we going?"

"I need a taste of you to get me through the night."

"Oh, Jeremy, that's very sweet. I'm more than happy to give you a kiss."

He pushes me up against a wall in a deserted wing of the house. He takes my mouth hungrily, kissing and licking me, driving me out of my mind. He stops and drops to his knees. "What are you doing?"

"Though I love those luscious lips, that wasn't the taste I was talking about."

"Oh. Jeremy! We can't do that here," I whisper loudly.

"Watch me," he says as he gets underneath my voluminous dress. He moves my panties aside and devours my pussy like he needs it to survive. I hold onto the wall to keep my balance as he pushes one finger in, then another. Soon, he is taking turns fucking me with his tongue and his fingers. The pleasure is too intense. I clamp my hand over my mouth to hold in a scream as I come so hard, my legs nearly give out. I gush all over his face and fingers. He's still under my skirt. I can hear him lapping up every drop of liquid.

Finally, he stands and kisses my mouth again. I taste the tanginess of my release on him. It turns me on even more that he seems so starved for me.

"Okay, beautiful. That should last me for a little while. Let's enjoy the ball for a bit, then I'll take you home with me and we'll spend the rest of the night enjoying each other."

Yesss! As lovely as this ball is, I would love to fast forward to the going home part. As we walk back to the ballroom, he takes me in his arms and guides me through a shockingly graceful waltz. It's hard to believe such a large man can move so fluidly.

"You are a great dancer."

He grins. "You can thank my mother for that. She made me take lessons when I was in school."

After a few dances, he goes to get us drinks. I'm watching everyone dance when a guy from our office approaches me. Darrin, I think. He starts small talking, then talking about work. That's the last thing I want to do right now. I assume he's just being friendly, until he asks me to dance. When I politely refuse, he tries to pull me into his arms. I do my best to push him away from me, but he won't let me go. "Stop it!" I yell.

The next thing I know, he drops like a rock. I turn around to see Jeremy rubbing his knuckles and looking really pissed. "Never. Touch. Her. Again," he enunciates each word quietly and angrily. Darrin nods his head and races out of the room.

"That was a little bit of overkill, don't you think?" I say, breathlessly, even though, to be honest, I thought it was hot as hell. My drenched panties can attest to that.

"No one touches you but me." He growls, then tosses me over his shoulder and yells, "mine!" He smacks my ass and heads out the door with me holding onto him.

I gently pound my fists against his back, enjoying this way more than I should. "How dare you manhandle me, you brute! Put me down, you Neanderthal!" I'm lightly fighting, but I'm incredibly turned on by this show of possession, even though I know I shouldn't be. I see Ella looking at me, wide-eyed. I wink to let her know that I am totally good with being kidnapped by Jeremy.

"Where are we going? What are we doing?"

He tosses me in the backseat of the limo, and slams the door shut. "I'm claiming what's mine," he says before devouring my mouth in a kiss so hot, it makes my toes curl.

Jeremy

♥

I take her puffy lips over and over again. I'm staking my claim on this woman right here and now. "You are mine!" I roar. I'm acting insane, but when I saw Darrin touching her, I fucking lost it. She is mine and mine alone. No other man had better touch her. Ever.

The partition is up, so the driver can't see or hear us. Thank God, because I am about to defile my beautiful girl in the back of this limo. I should wait until we get to my place, but I can't make it that long. I need her. Now.

I push the front of her dress down, and immediately suck her diamond hard nipple into my mouth, making her mewl. I suck the other one, taking turns to give both sides attention. I squeeze and pinch her big breasts before sucking on her neck, which I know will leave a mark. That shouldn't make me so happy, but it really fucking does. I want everyone to know that she belongs to me; especially her.

I push up her dress again. This time, I rip her panties off before shoving my face back against her dripping cunt. "Jeremy!" she screams. I lick and fuck her with my tongue until she can't take any more. I eat her sweet pussy through three orgasms before she pushes me away. "Too much," she breathes.

"Not enough," I correct her. I unzip my pants, freeing my painfully hard erection. "I'm claiming you right now. You are fucking mine, Shelly. You belong to me. I'm going to fuck you over and over again until you know that without a doubt."

Shelly

♥

"Yes!" My mouth waters as I stare in fascination at his huge cock. *Damn!* I knew he was packing, but his dick makes porn star dicks look tiny. He's already given me a ton of orgasms, but I am desperate to feel him inside me. I just hope I can take all of him.

"I'm yours, Jeremy. Fuck me. Show me that I belong to you."

He growls and slams in all the way with one hard thrust. I feel a slight tear, then nothing but bliss. He holds us both still. "Are you okay, baby? Why didn't you tell me?" he places gentle kisses on my cheeks and lips.

"Because I didn't want you to stop. It only hurt for a second. It feels so good now. Please, Jeremy. Don't stop. Fuck me like you want to."

I can tell he is trying to hold himself back. He starts off taking me slowly. After a few minutes, though, he loses control. My hips thrust up toward him, seeking more. He fucks me so hard, I spiral into orgasm after orgasm as he hits a magical spot inside me I never knew existed.

"Fuck, baby. You feel so fucking good. Your sweet little pussy is so tight and hot. Gonna fuck it every day."

"Yes!" I scream. I dig my fingernails into his back, then grab his firm ass and grind my pussy against his cock, pushing him even further inside me.

"Baby, you feel so good, I can't hold on anymore. I'm gonna fill you up with cum and put my baby in you."

"Oh, God!" I let go and come again and again. My contractions set off his. He roars as he empties himself inside me. After several minutes, he straightens our clothes and hugs me against him while we both do our best to catch our breath.

Jeremy

♥

When the limo pulls up to my house, I carry my woman bridal style into my home, which will soon be hers, if I have any say in it. I take her through the house and up to my bedroom. I unzip her dress, and unwrap the loveliest present ever.

She smiles coyly at me before lying back on the bed. I spend several seconds admiring her gorgeous, naked body. Her juicy tits and wide hips are perfect. She is perfect. Perfect for fucking, and perfect for having my babies.

She motions with her finger for me to come closer. I discard my clothes in record time before covering her sexy body once again with mine.

I kiss her mouth, then spend a few minutes kissing her neck, breasts, stomach, and legs, before zeroing in on her precious pussy again. I spend several minutes there, getting us both revved up, before slamming my cock back inside the heaven that is her sweet cunt. Mine! She is mine.

I slam into her harder and harder, claiming her, and ruining her for anyone else. Only I can give her the pleasure she needs, just like she's the only one who can give it to me. I fuck into her a few more times before her hot little pussy clamps down on my cock like a vise. I roar my release again. I come and come, hoping that I've knocked my woman up.

I get a damp cloth to clean both of us up. By the time I'm finished, Shelly has already nodded off. I pull her body against mine, and throw the covers over us. Snuggled up against her, I fall almost instantly into a deep sleep.

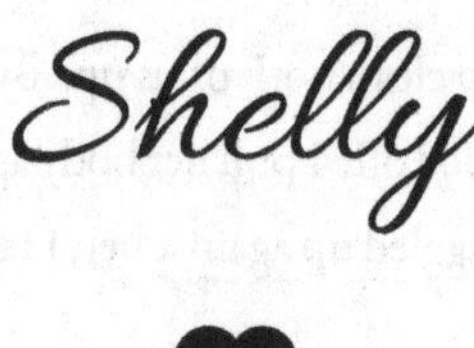

Shelly

I guess I must have dozed off. The last thing I remember is Jeremy cleaning me up. I awaken to total darkness and feel a very hard cock grinding against my ass. Jeremy's fingers stroke my pussy. The wet, slurping sounds fill the silent room. "I need you again, baby."

"Yes," I whisper. I'm still half asleep, but I don't care. I want to feel him inside me again. This time, he pulls me on top of him. He thrusts all the way in, making me cry out with pleasure. I ride him hard, seeking the unearthly release that he gave me earlier. "More! Harder!"

He takes control, even though I'm on top. He slams me down hard on his cock. He's hitting my clit every time, building up to a huge explosion. I feel myself clamp down on him as I come hard, drenching the bed. He explodes inside me at the same time. I swear, I see stars.

He fucks me three more times during the night. Once on all fours, once against the wall, and once on our sides. Each time is even better and more mind blowing than the time before. I'm still dead to the world when I wake up to him lapping at my pussy once again. Within minutes, I'm ready for his big cock. We spend several hours enjoying each other before Prince interrupts us.

Jeremy

♥

Prince calls late in the day, interrupting our time together. If it was anyone else, I probably wouldn't answer, but he is my friend and boss, so I do. "Hello," I say, putting him on speakerphone so I can still caress my woman.

"Hey, Jeremy. Sorry to bother you, but I need to know how to reach your assistant."

I can't stop the growl that comes out of me. Mine! "Why do you need to get a hold of her?"

"Because I'm marrying Ella and she has disappeared."

"What?" Shelly yells. "Give me the phone, you Neanderthal. You're marrying her? What do you mean she has disappeared?"

"I had to go out of town for a meeting. She was supposed to go get Cujo, then pack some stuff and go back to my house. She never showed and she's not answering my calls or messages."

"That's really not like her. I bet that bitch of a stepmom has done something to her. I'll go over there right now!"

"The hell you will, sweetheart," I say in a tone that brooks no argument.

"She's my best friend!"

"And you are my woman. Where you go, I go."

"Okay, fine."

"I touch down in fifteen minutes. Meet me at the airport and we'll all go together."

Shelly is pacing back and forth and biting her fingernails. The tears in her eyes nearly gut me. I hang up with Prince and give her a reassuring hug. "Everything will be okay, sweetheart. I promise."

"It better be, or I'll murder her evil stepmother."

I quickly throw one of my shirts on her that hangs down far enough to look like a dress. She looks adorable. The choices were that or her ball gown, so this works. The two of us dress quickly and race off to meet Prince at the airport.

Shelly

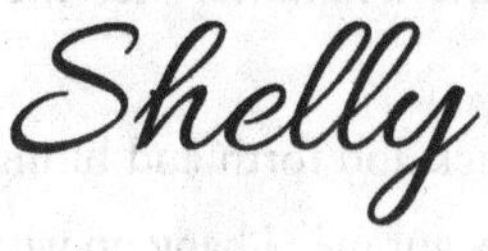

When we get to Ella's, the three of us pound on the door and are greeted by her stepmonster. "The evil stepmom, I presume?" Prince asks.

"Excuse me? My name is Katherine James and this is my house. How may I help you?"

"You can bring Ella to the door before all hell breaks loose."

"Ella? She's not here. She left to marry my son, Ken."

"Not a fucking chance," I fume. "This cunt is lying. Ken makes Ella's skin crawl."

"Not to mention that she's already engaged to me," Prince tells the woman glaring at us.

"Hey. What's that noise?" Jeremy asks. We all listen for a moment.

"It's Cujo!" Prince and I say in unison.

"Ella left him here so she and Ken could have some alone time."

I look at Prince and Jeremy. "No way. She never leaves him here when she's gone. She always brings him to me or my mom because she doesn't trust either one of them with him," I say confidently.

"Look, lady. You'd better back the fuck up and let us in," Prince pushes her aside and storms in. "Ella! Ella, where are you, baby?"

"What's going on?" Ken asks as he walks in.

"Ken, I presume? Funny. I thought you and Ella were off getting married," Prince says, moving closer to him.

"Um, yeah. I just came back for a second. She's at the courthouse, waiting for me."

Prince goes haywire. "Bullshit! You'd better tell me where she is right this second or you are a dead man." He slams Ken against the wall, crushing his windpipe with his arm.

"I'm calling the police!" Katherine yells.

"That's great. Tell the chief I said hi," Prince says menacingly.

He is cutting off Ken's air supply to get him to talk. Finally, he does. "Okay, okay. She's in the dungeon."

"Where the hell is that? Take me to it. Jeremy, watch the bitch. Ella had better be unharmed or neither of you will live to see another day."

Ken leads him down to the basement. I stay with Jeremy for a couple of minutes, but I have to make sure Ella is safe. She is my bestie, and the sweetest person in the world. She doesn't deserve whatever the hell these two fuckwads had planned for her.

As I get closer, I hear a lot of yelling. I peek in and see Ken pointing a gun at Prince. I look around for a weapon, and see some loose bricks lying in the hall. I grab one and whack Ken on the back of the head with it. Between me, Cujo, and Prince attacking him at once, Ken goes down. Ella is safe. Thank God!

Jeremy

♥

Since I was watching Katherine upstairs, I missed all the action down in the dungeon. It's probably a good thing I did. Shelly risked her life to save her friend. I'll have to punish her for scaring the crap out of me. I drive us home in silence. "You seem upset. Are you mad about something?" she asks quietly.

I pull the car into the drive and turn to look at her. "Baby, you scared me to death. He could have killed you."

"And he could have killed Ella! In fact, he planned to."

"I know, baby. I know. And I understand why you did what you did, but you have to understand where I'm coming from. The thought of losing you is more than I can bear. I love you so much, Shelly. I don't ever want to lose you."

"Oh, Jeremy. I don't ever want to lose you either." She pauses for a moment. "Wait a minute. Did you just say you love me?"

"Of course, baby. I thought you knew that."

"Well, I knew you liked me and wanted me, but I didn't know that you loved me." She places a gentle kiss on my mouth. "By the way, I love you, too."

"Thank God! So, marry me."

"Excuse me?"

"Marry me. I'm head over heels in love with you, and have been since I first laid eyes on you. You are it for me, baby, and I want our life together to start as soon as possible."

She looks at me like I'm crazy, but I see tears in her eyes. "This is crazy. You know that, right?" I nod my head. "Yes! I love you so much! I will marry you."

I smile at her. "Let me take you inside and show you how much I love you."

"Please do."

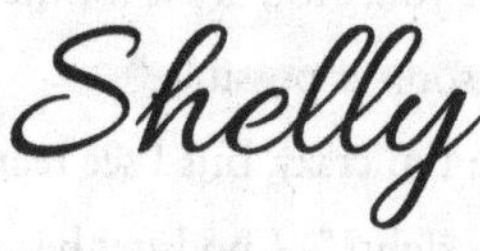

Shelly

A few hours later, Ella and Prince call us. "We're getting married tomorrow!" they yell in unison.

"What? Oh my God! Congratulations!"

Ella's voice comes through the phone. "Thank you. Shelly, I know we always talked about having a double wedding, but I don't want to wait. With everything that has happened, I realize how precious life is. I don't want to wait a minute longer to marry Prince."

"I totally understand. Not to steal your thunder, but we are engaged, too!"

"No way!" Ella's scream can probably be heard down the street. I look up to see Jeremy staring at me with a question in his eyes.

"We'll call you guys back in just a minute," he says, turning to me. "Baby, do you want to get married tomorrow?"

I feel tears running down my cheeks. "Yes, but I didn't want to rush you."

"Sweetheart, I was ready to marry you the first time I saw you. It can't happen soon enough for me."

He hugs me tightly to him. We call our friends back. "So guys, there's been a slight change of plans for tomorrow..."

Shelly

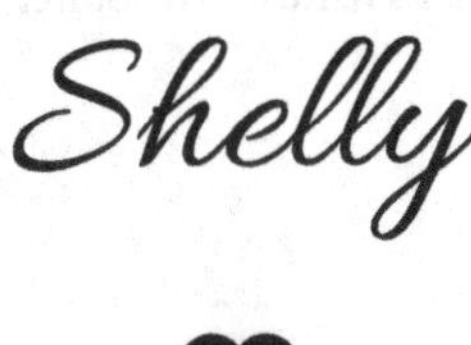

It's the day of our double wedding. Prince and Jeremy called in some serious favors to get a gorgeous venue-The Brownstone Hotel. It's one of the oldest, most elegant hotels in the city. I've heard the wait list for a wedding here is two years or more, but our men managed to get it in one day.

The sweet little lady from *Your Fairy Godmother* brought us several gorgeous gowns to choose from. Any of them would have been lovely, but we each found one that was perfect for us.

We have spent the day finding dresses, and going to the hotel spa to be pampered and beautified. Everyone I love is here-Jeremy, Mom, Ella, and even Cujo. Jeremy's mom is here, too. She is the sweetest lady ever. She came in earlier, hugged me, and loaned me a beautiful necklace of hers as my something borrowed. She is so excited that her son has found someone. Neither of our moms seem fazed that we are getting married so quickly.

Ella and I finish fixing each others veils, trying not to cry. "Can you believe this?" she asks. "We were both single just a few days ago."

I laugh. "I know. We both landed the men of our dreams at a fairy tale ball. How cool is that? Maybe our fairy godmother really knew what she was talking about."

My mom pops her head in. "Are you ladies ready?"
We squeeze each other's hands. "Absolutely!"

Jeremy

♥

I stand at the end of the aisle, waiting for Shelly to appear. When she finally does, everything around me fades into the background. There has never been a more beautiful bride. Her mother walks both the girls up the aisle. Tears threaten to drop from her eyes, but I can tell she is happy for both of them. I'm glad Shelly was blessed with a mother who loves her so much, just as I was.

When she is finally standing beside me, I feel a sense of calm wash over me. I kiss her hand, then her neck, before taking her mouth for several long seconds. The minister clearing his throat brings me back to reality, and keeps me from doing something I shouldn't in a room full of people.

We say our vows, along with Prince and Ella. When it's finally time to kiss my bride, I don't hold back. I take her mouth again and again, leaving us both gasping for air. "Time to go to our room, sweetheart," I whisper against her ear before tossing her over my shoulder, causing her to giggle.

"Jeremy! Why are we leaving?" she whispers.

"We're going upstairs so I can fuck my wife properly."

"Oh," she says quietly, "when you put it that way, okay."

I notice Prince had the same idea. The girls hug each other over our shoulders before we go to our respective rooms.

❦

Shelly

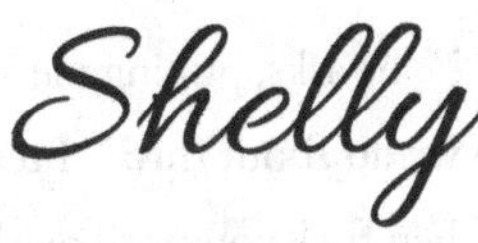

Jeremy carries me over the threshold of our hotel room before slowly sliding me down his body. I'm so busy looking at him, it takes me a few minutes to notice our suite.

"Oh, Jeremy! This is beautiful!" There's a huge living room with a giant, fluffy white sofa and cushy carpet. He steers me into the bedroom, which is dominated by a huge four poster bed. Rose petals are scattered across it, making a heart. "How sweet! I love it!"

He shows me the bathroom, which has a jacuzzi tub for two. It is already filled with steaming water and rose petals. I turn and hug my extremely thoughtful husband. "I can't believe you did all of this."

"Don't you know by now? I would do anything for you, baby." He leans down and kisses me tenderly before backing me into the bedroom. "If you don't want this shredded, you'd better show me how to unzip it." I show him the zipper on the side of my dress. He pulls it down slowly, setting my skin on fire with his touch as he goes.

I step out of my dress and place it gently on a chair. When I turn back around, my new husband is licking his lips and adjusting his very hard cock. It is pushing against his pants, trying to get to me.

"Jesus, you look beautiful, baby. Come here." I make my way over to him, putting a little extra sway in my hips.

"You like?" I ask, twirling around to give him a view of my sexy wedding lingerie.

"What do you think?" he asks, pulling me against his hardness.

"Oh, my. What can we do about this?" I tease.

"I'm going to strip, then fuck you until neither of us can move."

"Ooh. Promises, promises."

Jeremy manages to strip down to nothing in just a few seconds. He doesn't look like the calm, cool businessman that everyone else knows. He looks like a predator about to devour his prey. His gaze caresses me from head to toe, setting my nerve endings on fire.

I drop to my knees, and lick the head of his cock like a lollipop. "Mmm. You taste so good." He grabs my hair and starts thrusting in my mouth.

"Damn, baby. Your hot little mouth is heaven." He thrusts harder, as I rub my clit, trying to get some relief from the throbbing need I have. "Enough," he says, pulling me up.

He pulls me against his naked body, taking my mouth like he can't get enough of it, before dropping us both onto the bed. "You look gorgeous, sweetheart, but I need you naked. Now." With that, he rips my lingerie off of me, completely destroying it.

"I can't believe you did that," I start to protest as he slams all the way inside me, causing me to clench around him, immediately coming.

"What was that, sweetheart?" he asks, thrusting harder and harder.

"Oh, God. Nothing. Just don't stop."

"Not a fucking chance. Come for me, sweetheart," he says as he plays with my clit, while kissing my neck and slamming inside me again and again. I spiral; screaming his name. My orgasm sets off his. He comes hard inside me, drenching me with his cum.

He carries me to the bath, where we wash each other and snuggle until the water starts to cool and our skin turns pruny. After drying each other off, he tosses me back onto the bed, where he takes me several more times throughout the night. He keeps his promise. By the time the morning rolls around, we are both too tired to move. *Best wedding night ever!*

Epilogue-Jeremy

♥

Two months later...

"Mr. Strong? Do you have a few minutes for me?"

"Of course, Shelly. I always have time for you." I smile as she closes the door and locks it behind her. When my wife calls me Mr. Strong, I know it's playtime. "What can I do for you?"

"Well," she says nervously, "I seem to have an unbearable ache between my legs. I'm hoping you can help me with it."

"Fuck yeah, I can," I say as my cock hardens to full mast. "Come here, sweetheart. I'm really hungry. I'd like something to eat."

"Oh, Mr. Strong, I don't think we have anything in here to eat."

"Come sit on my desk, Shelly."

"Okay," she says demurely.

"Now pull up your skirt and spread your legs for me."

"Oh, sir. I don't think I should do that."

"And I think you should. Do it now." She does as I say, lying down on my desk, and showing me her bare, dripping pussy. "No underwear? Fuck, baby. If I would have known you were bare under there, I never would have made it through the day." I dive in, devouring her sweet little cunt with my lips and tongue.

I make her come on my mouth twice before pulling away. "That felt so good, Mr. Strong. I still feel empty, though."

"Not for long," I growl as I undo my slacks and slam my hard cock inside her dripping hot cunt. We started out playing, but now I'm out of control, fucking my wife as hard as I can. I flip her around, bending her over my desk as I fuck her so hard, my heavy desk starts inching across the floor.

"Yes! Just like that! More! Harder!"

I fuck her harder, grabbing her plump tits. After a few minutes, she cries out again, coming hard. Her tight heat pulses around me, making me spill inside her. I straighten our clothes and sit down in my chair, pulling my beautiful wife onto my lap. We spend a few minutes catching our breath.

"You have no idea how many times I envisioned bending you over my desk and fucking the hell out of you before we got together."

She laughs. "Me, too. The good news is now you can do it whenever you want. At least, during non-working hours."

I kiss her tenderly. "You've given me so much, sweetheart. Is there anything you want that I can give you? Just name it and it's yours."

"Well, there is something, but you've already given it to me." I look at her in confusion. "Just a sec. I brought you a present." She grabs a little box out of her purse and hands it to me.

I open it, not sure what to expect. When I see a white plastic stick with the word "pregnant" spelled out, I feel tears rolling down my cheeks. "Are you happy?" she asks.

"Oh, sweetheart. Of course I am. I'm over the moon. In case you haven't noticed, I've been doing my best to knock you up since the moment we got together. This is the best present anyone has ever given me." I kiss her again. I can't believe we are having a baby. We definitely need to call our moms. They will be thrilled. Our little one will grow up with so many people that love him or her.

I have a wife that I love beyond belief. I didn't think anything could make me any happier until I saw that test. Our little family will be complete. I am so thankful that this beautiful woman came to work at our company. I can't imagine my life without her.

Epilogue-Shelly

❤

Two years later...

"What have you two gotten into?" I swear, all I did was go in the living room for a few seconds. In that time, Sable and Sage have somehow managed to have a baby food fight. They both giggle adorably, but they are both covered in green goo. Gross.

"I'm home!" Jeremy calls as he comes in the door. As he spots the twins, he comes to a halt, then laughs hysterically. "How did this happen?" he asks before giving me a quick kiss.

"I have no idea! I walked out of the room for a few seconds." I pout. Seriously, these two keep us on our toes. The messes they make are unbelievable.

"How about I help you wrangle them into the bathtub before Ella and Prince get here." They are bringing little Emory over in a bit for a play date. Our kids were born less than a week apart, so they are growing up together. It works out great for all of us. The seven of us spend tons of time together.

My plan to take over the business world has been placed on a temporary hold. I decided to stay home with the kids until they start school. I can't stand the idea of being away from my babies every day while they are so young.

I helped Jeremy find an awesome assistant to take my place. Brandon is fabulous. I'm a jealous bitch, so I wasn't about to have some hot chick trying to hit on my man.

After a very messy bath time, the kids go down easily for their afternoon nap. We are both soaked. We definitely need to change clothes. I start stripping as I walk. He does the same.

"Now, Mrs. Strong. What should we do while the kids are sleeping?"

I pretend to think. "Hmmm. Watch a movie? Do some gardening?" I laugh as he nibbles on my neck.

"I think you know that's not what I had in mind." He tosses me over his shoulder and heads down the hall to our bedroom. "I think I need to remind you who you belong to." And he does, twice, before the kids wake up.

Jeremy is the best husband and father a girl could ask for. I'm so lucky that he's mine, but he would tell you it's the other way around. Our house is full of love for each other, and for our beautiful, mischievous children. There's no place I'd rather be than here with the three of them. They are my happily ever after.

THE END

If you missed Prince and Ella's story, read Enticing Ella.

If you enjoyed these stories, please take a moment to leave a review. It is very helpful to newer authors like me. Thank you so much!

About the Author

♥

Lacy Jane is a happily married empty nester and dog mom who believes in happily ever afters and loves to write about them. She enjoys reading, streaming shows, hanging out with her husband, kids, friends, family, and dogs. She loves traveling, shopping, drinking delicious coffee drinks, and is a self-confessed beauty junkie. Her books are always OTT, high heat, instalove, no cheating, and (of course!) a HEA. Always a steamy read with HEA guaranteed.

Please sign up on my website to be notified of new books and freebies from time to time!

https://lacy-jane.mailchimpsites.com

http://www.amazon.com/author/lacyjane

https://www.facebook.com/author.lacy.jane

Also by Lacy Jane

♥

**The Obsessed Alphas Collection:
Books 5-8**

These four Obsessed Alphas stories turn up the heat! Each book features a strong heroine and a hero who won't stop until he has her. Each book is OTT with high heat, instalove, no cheating, and (of course!) a HEA. Always a steamy read with HEA guaranteed! Enjoy!

Includes four scorching hot books:
Claiming Callie
Taken by the CEO
Forbidden Passion
The Guardian's Temptation

https://www.amazon.com/dp/B0DDVPQH2F

Forbidden Attractions Series

Scorching hot, forbidden relationships!

These couples shouldn't be together because it's forbidden, but they just can't help themselves. Each is an extra-steamy, OTT, instalove, with extremely high heat, no cheating, and (of course!) a HEA. Always a steamy read with HEA guaranteed!

Wanting My Stepbrother

If you like extra-steamy, age gap romances, you'll love Wanting My Stepbrother!

Roman and Shelby meet and immediately fall head over heels for each other. Soon after, they find out that their parents just married each other, making them stepsiblings. A relationship between them is suddenly taboo. Why does that make it even hotter?

*They spend the next week sneaking around under their parents' roof, but something's got to give. It's so forbidden and **so good,** but how can it possibly last?*

This short, steamy read is OTT with extremely high heat, low drama, insta-everything, no cheating, and (of course!) a HEA. Always a steamy read with HEA guaranteed!

Wanting My Best Friend's Brother

Heather

I've been in love with Stan since I was a teenager. He's the only man I've ever wanted. I've worn out vibrators fantasizing about the sexy giant. He follows me everywhere, but I'm sure it's because he sees me as a little sister he needs to protect. But what if he wants me just as badly as I want him?

Stan

When I get out of the military, I find the woman of my dreams, but she's my little sister's best friend. I promise her I will leave Heather alone, but it's been six long months, and I'm more obsessed with her than ever. I spend every day watching her, protecting her, stalking her, wanting her. I've never wanted anything as badly as I want Heather. I feel my control slipping a little more every day. When someone dares lay their hands on my girl, I lose all semblance of control. There's no turning back now. It's time to finally make her mine.

This series is set in Cedar Falls, the same place as my Tempting Treats series. This extra-steamy age gap romance is OTT with high heat, instalove, no cheating, and (of course!) a HEA. Always a steamy read with HEA guaranteed!

Snowed in with Temptation

Laney has fought her attraction to Dante since meeting him, but when they get snowed in together, will she finally give in to the red hot desire between them? Sparks fly between an older, sexy attorney and his business partners' gorgeous daughter in this extra-steamy, forced proximity romance.

Laney

Dante is business partners with my parents, and much closer to their age than mine. He is also tall, dark, sexy as hell, and totally irresistible. Staying away from him is pretty difficult since we work together and every touch from him sends my body up in flames. When we get snowed in together in a remote cabin with only one bed, I know I won't be able to resist him any longer.

Dante

As soon as I saw Laney, I knew she was mine. There are several reasons I shouldn't claim my baby girl-she's way too young, I'm friends and business partners with her parents, and she works for me. But none of that matters. I will make her mine; consequences be damned.

Like all of my books, this OTT romance has high heat, in-stalove, no cheating, and (of course!) a HEA. Always a steamy read with HEA guaranteed!

The Tempting Treats Collection
https://www.amazon.com/dp/B0D6LFKPKJ

Cute, extra-steamy, OTT, instalove short stories, set in a small town.

The Abbott triplets move to Cedar Falls, Montana to open their bakery, Tempting Treats. Little do they know that they are each about to meet the man of their dreams. Meet Aurora, Avery, and Audrey and enjoy their hot, whirlwind romances! This series is sweet, steamy, and OTT with high heat, instalove, no cheating, and (of course!) a HEA. Always a steamy read with HEA guaranteed! Enjoy!

Sweets for the Sheriff

The first book in my new Tempting Treats series!
Aurora Abbott is the most tempting treat Sheriff Garrison James has ever seen. He is instantly smitten with the sexy little baker, and is determined to make her his. The chemistry between them is undeniable, and it's not long before passion ignites.

As their whirlwind romance heats up, Aurora finds herself falling hard for the sexy sheriff, but is overcome with fear and uncertainty. Can Garrison push past her walls and make her his, permanently?

Hudson's Sweet Honey

Can a steamy night with a stranger turn into happily ever after? Find out in this racy, instalove romance.

When Hudson meets Avery, he instantly knows she is the one, but she assumes he doesn't want anything serious. After an unforgettable night of passion, he knows he will never let her go. She is his. He just needs to convince his little goddess that he's all in. How will he accomplish that? By putting a baby in her belly and a ring on her finger.

Cupcakes for Colton

When Audrey takes a stray dog to the vet, she comes face to face with a seriously hot veterinarian and his package that she can't take her eyes off of. After a funny, steamy, meet cute, Colton vows to do whatever it takes to make this awkward, adorable woman his for life.

These three stories are extra-steamy, fun, and sweet. You'll swoon over these three sexy heroes who win the Abbott sisters' hearts!

https://www.amazon.com/dp/B0D6LFKPKJ

Once Upon a Time: Twisted Sexy Fairy Tales Volume 1: (Books 1-3)

https://www.amazon.com/dp/B0C2DJJHHK

The first three books of Once Upon a Time: Twisted Sexy Fairy Tales:

Goldie Locks and the Three Sexy Bear Shifters

Little Red and the Big, Bad, Sexy Wolf

Enticing Ella

Get these three sexy fairy tales in one book!

Goldie Locks and the Three Sexy Bear Shifters: A Steamy Reverse Harem Romance: (Once Upon a Time: Twisted Sexy Fairy Tales-Book 1)

https://www.amazon.com/dp/B0B9317SMP

Once upon a time, there was a girl named Goldie Locks who had very sexy dreams...

Every night, Goldie has dreams about her fated mates-three sexy bear shifters, but wakes every morning alone and longing for them. When she finally finds her beasts, they are ravenous for her. The sexy, possessive brothers will show her what it's like to be loved by three passionate shifters who are obsessed with their mate.

This very adult fairy tale is hot, hot, hot! If you prefer your romances sweet and squeaky clean, this is not the book for you, but if you like your romances racy and sexy, this is right up your alley. Three sexy shifters, a strong heroine who knows what she wants, and (of course!) a HEA. My books are for those who like their happily ever after a little on the dirty side. A steamy read with HEA guaranteed. Enjoy!

Little Red and the Big, Bad, Sexy Wolf: (Once Upon a Time: Twisted Sexy Fairy Tales-Book 2)

When shifter Damian Wolf meets Scarlett, he'll stop at nothing, including using their uncontrollable attraction to each other, to make her his. Will the big, bad, sexy wolf and his human fated mate get their happily ever after? Find out in this modern, sexy take on Little Red Riding Hood.

This very adult fairy tale is hot, hot, hot! If you prefer your romances sweet and squeaky clean, this is not the book for you. On the other hand, if you like racy, steamy romances with sexy heroes and strong heroines, this is right up your alley.

This is the second book in my series Once Upon a Time: Twisted Sexy Fairy Tales. Each book is a stand alone, though characters from the other stories occasionally make appearances. As always, this book has high heat, no cheating, instalove, and (of course!) a HEA.

My books are for those who like their happily ever after a little on the dirty side. Always a steamy read with HEA guaranteed. Enjoy!

Enticing Ella (A Billionaire, Older Man, Younger Woman, Steamy Short): Once Upon a Time: Twisted Sexy Fairy Tales Book 3

After a night of passion with Prince, Ella disappears. Now that he has claimed her, Prince will stop at nothing to find Ella and make her his bride. Can he save her from her evil stepmother in time? Find out in this sweet, spicy, modern version of Cinderella, complete with a ball, one evil stepmother, a fairy godmother of sorts, and Ella's adorable little dog, Cujo.

As with all of my books, this contains high heat, instalove, no cheating, and (of course!) a HEA. My books are always a steamy read with HEA guaranteed! Enjoy!

* 9 7 9 8 3 3 0 3 6 9 6 4 5 *